KIDNAPPING IN HOPE TOWN

NICOLE HELM

Harlequin

INTRIGUE

To my phone obsessed teen.

 Harlequin® INTRIGUE™

Recycling programs for this product may not exist in your area.

ISBN-13: 978-1-335-69075-3

Kidnapping in Hope Town

 Harlequin Enterprises ULC
22 Adelaide St. West, 41st Floor
Toronto, Ontario M5H 4E3, Canada
www.Harlequin.com

HarperCollins Publishers
Macken House, 39/40 Mayor Street Upper,
Dublin 1, D01 C9W8, Ireland
www.HarperCollins.com

Printed in Lithuania

1 2 3 4 5 6 7 8 9 10 LIT 28 27 26 25

Gard took Lia by the arm and began ushering her out of the theater.

"Can Albennie come pick you up? Or Franny? Hell, I can call Royal and—"

"I'm coming with you, Gard."

"You can't come with, Lia."

"I have to," she replied stubbornly. "I know what you need to look for and look out for. I'm the best chance you've got."

Yeah, he really wanted to know *how*, but he didn't have time. "This is police business."

"You're not going as a cop. You're going as an uncle. And a brother. Which means it's not police business for you. Which means I'm going *with* you."

"I'm going with a *gun*."

"You can leave me here, but I'll only follow. You can't cut me out of this. It's too important, and I offer too much."

He reached out, cupped her face with his hands. "How am I supposed to save them if I have to worry about you?"

Nicole Helm grew up with her nose in a book and the dream of one day becoming a writer. Luckily, after a few failed career choices, she gets to follow that dream—writing down-to-earth contemporary romance and romantic suspense. From farmers to cowboys, Midwest to the West, Nicole writes stories about people finding themselves and finding love in the process. She lives in Missouri with her husband and two sons, and dreams of someday owning a barn.

Books by Nicole Helm

Harlequin Intrigue

Hope Town Secrets

Kidnapping in Hope Town

Bent County Protectors

Vanishing Point
Killer on the Homestead
Fatal Deception
Eyewitness in Danger

Hudson Sibling Solutions

Cold Case Kidnapping
Cold Case Identity
Cold Case Investigation
Cold Case Scandal
Cold Case Protection
Cold Case Discovery
Cold Case Murder Mystery

Visit the Author Profile page at Harlequin.com.

CAST OF CHARACTERS

Corporal Gardner "Gard" Fairhurst—Corporal and field training officer at Bent County Sheriff's Department.

Lia Blair—Manager of the Hope Town Bakery.

Sammy Fairhurst—Gard's niece who he sometimes acts as guardian of.

Dani Fairhurst—Sammy's mom and Gard's sister.

Albennie Ward—Lia's assistant manager at Hope Town Bakery and her friend.

Zach Simmons—Creator of Hope Town. Married to Lucy (who is also country singer Daisy Delaney).

Sarabeth Thompson & Izzy Hudson—Sammy's friends from school.

Franny Perkins—Lives above the bakery and is friends with Lia and is dating Deputy Royal Campbell.

Deputy Royal Campbell—Deputy with the Bent County Sheriff's Department who was trained by Gard.

Chapter One

Corporal Gardner Fairhurst had his life down to a perfect science these days. He had a challenging, fulfilling job. One that offered him enough spontaneity and movement to serve the side of him that craved both, without drawing him into the kinds of danger he'd been trying to pull his younger sister out of since he could remember.

Maybe being a cop hadn't turned out to be as *save the world* as he'd once thought when he'd been young and eager and naive, but he still knew that he helped people. On the bad days, it felt like not enough. On the good days, it felt like a badge of honor he'd earned.

Tonight, he'd clocked out, radioed off duty, and headed inside his nice little house on Main Street in Bent, Wyoming. Today had neither been good nor bad, and after some of the years of *bad* he'd been through, he appreciated a boring day that offered neither.

Or maybe he was just getting old. Sure, forty was a few years off yet, but it was breathing down his neck. Something he was reminded of with each new recruit he was assigned to train who seemed to get younger and younger with each assignment.

A couple of the *kids*, as he called them, had invited him to hit Rightful Claim, the local saloon in Bent. Gard had declined. Tonight, he'd shower. Eat a frozen dinner and watch a sporting event. Then go to bed. Alone.

Some people might call it boring, but Gard figured those people had never spent time in the unknown. They'd never turned their back on everything comfortable and supportive and easy and then had to suddenly rebuild their own life.

Boring was a death knell only for people who'd never known *struggle*.

Besides, going out when you were feeling your age was a recipe for recklessness and disaster, so Gard stayed in. Recklessness wasn't his MO.

He ran through the shower, microwaved a frozen chicken potpie, and grabbed a beer from his fridge. He was halfway to the couch when he heard a noise outside his front door. The knob of said door moved. He stood, beer in one hand, a microwaved chicken potpie on a plate in the other. He'd locked that door—a habit being a cop had ingrained deep into his bones. Still, the knob jiggled and moved and then…opened.

He blew out a breath and scowled at the intruder. "Sammy."

His niece stepped inside. She'd dyed her usually blond hair black since the last time he'd seen her a few weeks ago, and she had it piled on top of her head in messy waves. Her blue eyes were direct and defiant, reminding Gard of her mother. She had a duffel bag slung over her shoulder.

And there was no one entering his house with her.

So just like that, the well-ordered construct of his world crumbled. Because if Sammy was here without her mother…

"Just to get it out of the way, she never came home last night," Sammy said, her voice devoid of all emotion except generic teenage distaste for everything. "I don't know where she is, and since she didn't come back *tonight*, I guess I'm crashing here for a bit."

Gard didn't say anything to that at first. He'd bought this house with the extra bedroom for just this kind of situation, but… Things had been going so well, he'd really stopped thinking she'd need it.

"You want me in family services?" she demanded when he didn't say anything.

He sighed. He didn't *love* working around the system, but his sister had made that a constant struggle. Because the system kind of sucked when you couldn't stay clean, but you didn't want to lose your kid. Years ago, Gard had tried to convince Dani to give him custody—that way she wouldn't have to worry about the Department of Family Services.

Dani hadn't gone for it, and Gard hadn't felt right forcing the issue. And for the past three years, he hadn't even thought of it. Dani had been clean. Sammy had been good. *Everything* had been good. It killed him that after all this time, they were about to start over.

"Let me crash here," Sammy said, all world-weary detachment too big for a fifteen-year-old. "All you have to do is give me a ride to school in the mornings. I've got a ride home. No one will know the difference as long as I'm in school."

"You'll get a ride home from *who*?"

She smiled at him, reminding him so much of Dani it hurt. He'd never been able to save his sister, and he had increasing concern he'd never be able to save Sammy.

Sometimes a man had to accept people didn't want to be saved, but he'd never been able to accept that when it came to the people he loved.

"Don't worry about it," she said, tossing her lone duffel bag on his couch.

The problem was, he *did* worry about it. About Dani. About Sammy. He thought they were past her one-bagged arrivals. It had been three years since the last one, and back then it had always been Dani dropping Sammy off on her way to do something…bad.

Now, apparently, Sammy was old enough to show up all on her own. Even though she was still a few months shy from getting her driver's license.

"How'd you get here?" Dani and Sammy had a place in Fairmont. He'd had one too for a long time, but last year Dani had insisted she needed space. She needed to know she could take care of Sammy and herself without him breathing down her neck.

So he'd bought a house out here in Bent, about a half hour away. Space, but not…too much. Close enough, room enough, to be what either of them needed, if they needed.

"A friend dropped me off," Sammy said casually, but with a kind of smugness that made Gard especially aware he had no business helping raise a teenage girl.

But that was life. Gard was going to have to look into her friends. Which wouldn't win him any favors with Sammy, but he wasn't looking for her to hero-worship him like she had when she was little. He was desperate to find a way to help her be…all right.

God, he'd wanted that for his sister. And he hadn't given up on it, but this…hurt. He'd really thought she'd turned a corner. Three years. Three years clean without any problems. Why would she throw that away? "I thought…"

"We all think. We always think." Sammy walked into his kitchen, stuck her head into his fridge. "And she always goes back."

Her words were emotionless, but Gard knew better. Sammy might be resigned, but it wasn't like she hadn't found some hope these past few years either. Hope that was now dashed. Cruelly.

Gard hated that he couldn't argue with Sammy, couldn't find some way to protect that now-lost hope. "Here, eat this," he muttered, setting the potpie down on the table, and moving into the kitchen to make himself something else.

Lia Blair had never been a morning person. So the irony was not lost on her that she'd decided to run a bakery and coffee shop that necessitated her getting up before the sun just about every day.

Luckily, she'd hired a responsible assistant manager who often opened so Lia could get that extra hour of sleep in. But an extra hour of sleep in bakery world was still too damn early.

She could grumble about it, and would, but some mornings when she stepped out of her little house off the main drag of Hope Town, Wyoming, and the sunrise was a soft, pretty pastel painting on the sky, she was reminded of how lucky she was to be here.

It was a hell of a lot better than everything she'd endured as a teenager that had led her to a life in Hope Town's secret, privatized WitSec program.

Because her name might be Lia Blair here, but that was only because Edwina Cornelia Pitt didn't exist anymore. For her own protection. Something that didn't even faze her anymore. She liked her life here in Hope Town more than she'd ever liked any part of the life prior.

Since it was a nice day, and Lia planned on eating one of her giant cinnamon rolls for breakfast once she got into the bakery, she walked the short distance from house to bakery building out on Main Street rather than drive.

Albennie, her assistant manager, was already in the kitchen, doing the necessary first-thing-in-the-morning tasks. They didn't speak through that first hour—even in a good mood Lia wanted absolute silence before at least a cup and a half of coffee.

So, silently, Lia went through her first hour of work, frosting pastries, baking yesterday's doughs into rolls and the like. She drank her first cup of coffee as she worked, then sat down with her warm, delicious cinnamon roll and drank half the second cup.

Life was good.

The morning rush came through and kept Lia and Albennie busy, though not too rushed. Thursdays in Hope Town, Wyoming, weren't exactly teeming with people, but the threat of winter in the air had people getting out and about more than they would soon enough.

Things tapered off in the afternoon as they usually did. Albennie said her goodbyes, leaving Lia to clean up and close up once three finally hit. Since it was Thursday, the place was dead by two, but Lia stayed open, always ready for a straggler.

She used these downtimes to test new recipes or work on one of the million projects she was always working on to keep the historical building her bakery was in functioning. Today, she wasn't in the mood for tools or frustrating building-improvement projects, so she went to her kitchen.

She kept the music low so she could hear if someone came in—the bell on the door would ring. Then she lost herself in butter and sugar and the simple satisfaction she always felt when baking.

It *almost* made the early mornings worth it.

The new sugar cookie dough recipe she'd tried from an old cookbook she'd bought at the antique shop down the street was stickier than she'd like, messier than she'd like, but pretty darn tasty if she did say so herself.

She packaged it up to chill overnight then heard something…odd out in the front room. She wiped her hands on a towel and moved out of the kitchen area to the café itself.

There was someone inside. Which…didn't make sense since she hadn't heard the bell ring. But the figure stood on the other side of the counter. Not waiting to order, at least not if the open and empty cash register drawer was anything to go by.

From Lia's angle, she couldn't see their face or really make out much of them considering they were wearing an oversize, bulky hoodie.

She should probably pull her phone out of her pocket and call the Bent County Sheriff's Department, but she paused, watching as the figure helped themself to the money in the tip jar. They shoved it into their hoodie pocket, looked around—allowing Lia to see enough of their face for Lia to realize it was a girl. Probably a teenager.

The girl clearly didn't see Lia, because her next move was to reach around the counter, open the pastry display case at that awkward angle, and grab what she could.

Before the girl could fully pull her hand from the case, Lia took a step forward into her line of sight.

"Are you going to put that money back, or am I going to have to call the cops?" Lia hated cops. That would be a very, *very* last resort. But the threat when it came to teens usually worked.

Unless this teen was a lot like the teen she had been.

The girl stopped, though she didn't turn around to face

Lia. Lia imagined she was considering her chances of getting away if she ran.

Not good.

When the girl finally turned toward Lia, Lia blew out a breath. The eyes were blazing, the snarl combative. And there was that belligerence only a teen could pull out with such a lack of toughness behind it. She'd dropped the pastries and pretended she didn't see them on the floor. "I didn't take anything."

She couldn't be more than fifteen or sixteen. Full of bitterness and fury and helplessness. It was damn familiar. And the *last* thing Lia wanted to do was involve cops when she could so easily see herself being this girl.

But there was the way she wanted things to be, and the way things were. The food was one thing, but she could hardly let this girl just disappear with the money.

Zach Simmons might be cool with a lot of things, but he wasn't going to be down with that. Zach owned most of the buildings in Hope Town, funded pretty much all the businesses on start-up. Because he was the creator of the privatized WitSec in Hope Town, everything went through Zach.

Lia prided herself on turning a profit with her bakery. She prided herself on being *foundational* to Hope Town—what it was, what it stood for, whether anyone outside its inner circle knew those things or not.

Even if the girl needed the money, and she didn't strike Lia as someone who did based on what she was wearing, Lia couldn't just let her walk. Not and explain to Zach why her books were so out of whack.

Mostly because he'd likely *understand*, and worse, sympathize with her. Lia knew what had landed her in Hope Town. Knew her life was…well, *sad*. The few people who knew about all that sad were the few people she always wanted to prove to that she was *just fine* and *quite healed, thank you.*

"Put the money back on the counter," Lia said, trying to find a balance between gentle and firm. "We'll forget the food you took and the tray of cream puffs you ruined when you grabbed the food. No worries."

The girl snarled. Not great. Not smart. "I know my rights," the girl said.

Lia wanted to groan. There was no getting through to a person who *knew their rights*, especially a teenager. Which meant she had to do the thing she didn't want to do.

"Cops it is."

At least she knew the Bent County deputy assigned to Hope Town. She could probably work Royal around to warning the girl off in a way that gave her a bit of a *scare* and forced her to return the money without totally being a jerk about it.

God, she hoped.

Chapter Two

Gard didn't have anyone on field training right now, so he was enjoying being on the road by himself. He liked teaching and guiding the younger cops, but sometimes it was nice to exist in his own head. Like times when his sister had disappeared, and his niece was staying with him.

She'd assured him her friend, a *girl*, could drop her off at his house after school. Had *claimed* she had a Model UN meeting so she wouldn't be home much earlier than him—which he wasn't sure he was buying, but he didn't want to call her a liar. He could hardly *stalk* her. She was fifteen. She needed *some* autonomy.

And still her safety was the biggest thing. He didn't think she'd want to get involved with drugs after watching her mom struggle her whole life, but he knew young brains didn't always work in reasonable patterns.

He needed to find a babysitter. Someone Sammy liked and wouldn't think of *as* a babysitter. He didn't know how the hell he was going to accomplish that, but he needed to figure it out and fast. He had enough seniority to not work nights, and always had some days off built up, but he wouldn't be able to get out of every weekend and mandatory overtime was always a possibility.

Today, luckily, he was on Hope Town duty which was a

normal schedule. It'd get him off work and hopefully home around the same time as Sammy. The Hope Town duty required an afternoon walk up and down Main Street, just to show a police presence. There were plenty of shops, a smattering of tourists since it was a nice afternoon, and no trouble.

The assignment was usually boring and, again, that wasn't always a bad thing. Mostly, not much happened in Hope Town. There'd been a kidnapping a few months ago, but it had been taken care of.

Of course, after that dustup, Gard wasn't particularly sure everything that was going on in this town was on the up-and-up, but he didn't think it was necessarily…criminal. Exactly. Something about that kidnapping, about former FBI Agent Zach Simmons's involvement, and the way only women owned businesses in this place struck Gard as…*odd*.

Still, it was nice to get out of his cruiser, stretch his legs, and walk on a pretty afternoon. Smile at passersby. Hand out stickers to kids who seemed interested. All the while internally going through the list of people he knew who might have the time and inclination to keep their eye on a fifteen-year-old after school and on weekends when he had to work.

When the dispatcher called him on the radio, Gard was surprised to hear that there was a call at the Hope Town Bakery for him to respond to. A stealing in progress.

Surprising. But he was close, so he jogged down the street the rest of the way to the bakery. When he opened the door and stepped inside the sugary-smelling café, Lia Blair stood in the middle of the tables and chairs, arms crossed, mouth arranged in a scowl.

She was dressed as she usually was. Jeans. A Hope Town

Bakery T-shirt. Her dark hair pulled and pinned back behind a headband, no doubt in a nod to keep hair out of her baked goods. Her hazel eyes edged more green and flashed with annoyance.

The scowl did not change when she turned her gaze to him. If anything, it deepened. "I was hoping it would be Royal."

Gard didn't bristle, though it was a hard-won thing. Lia Blair had made her distaste from him known from their very first meeting—back when her bakery manager had been kidnapped and he'd had to question her.

He'd never known *why* she disliked him, but she'd made it clear. And continued to do so, any time they ran into each other—and since the Royal in question was one of his deputies and dating the woman who lived above the bakery, who just so happened to be friends with Lia, they did run into each other socially—not just in a cop-to-witness-questioning manner.

He'd tried to charm her. And then he'd used that charm to irritate her, because usually that kind of hostility rolled right off his shoulders. Lots of people didn't like cops or were weird about his profession, and that wasn't a reflection of him, so who cared?

Today, he was irritable, and he knew it was because he'd been up half the night trying to figure out where Dani would have gone. Usually she left clues. Usually, she at the very least texted him an apology. The fact she wasn't following the pattern left a hard ball of worry centered in his chest.

Worse, he *knew* better. Dani made her own choices, and yes, they were choices built on a foundation of trauma and substance abuse, but they were hers, and he needed to stop trying to absolve her of the consequences. If she'd bolted without a word, it wasn't out of the ordinary, it wasn't something he could *solve*. It was just her current choice.

But the worry persisted. The need to do something persisted. And it made it really hard not to be a jerk to Lia Blair's open hostility. But he was on duty so he let a slow breath out, forced himself to smile. "Campbell took off today. What seems to be the problem?"

"I've got a thief." She gestured to a girl in an oversize hoodie and…and a hoodie he recognized. Because it was *his* hoodie.

He had to close his eyes against the wave of frustration, helplessness, and—worst of all—grief. Because he didn't know what to do for his sister, and he was making all the same mistakes with his niece.

"Sammy, what is this?" he ground out.

"You know the thief?" Lia asked, with some level of surprise and not accusation.

Sammy smirked at the lady, a flash of Dani so potent Gard just wanted to haul her out of here, take her home, and lock her in his house until she got it through her head to stop repeating her mother's mistakes.

"Uncle Gard, tell this lady that I didn't take anything, and she can't prove I did."

Oh, if only he thought that were true. "Cut the crap, kid." He held out his hand. "Give me the money."

Her face went mutinous. "You don't believe me?" she shrieked.

"Give me the money," he repeated. He couldn't deal with the personal side of this just yet. First, he'd get Lia her money back, then he'd deal with…

God, he didn't know.

Sammy shoved her hand into the hoodie pocket, pulled

out a fistful of ones. She shoved it at him like he was the bad guy here.

He wished he could believe she was trying to help herself, but he just knew her too well. "All the money."

She looked at him with eyes full of hate and fury. Yeah, he'd had his fair share of that from Dani too. These days it didn't hurt so much as just make him *sad*. All he wanted to do was help, to save, to make things *okay*, but he could never seem to get that through to them. They just *had* to paint him as their enemy sometimes.

Sammy pulled out more money—a carefully folded wad of twenties. *Jesus*. He took it and handed it over to Lia. "Is that all of it?"

Lia counted it out. "Yeah, that's it." She looked up from the money, to Sammy, to him. There was something…calculating in her expression. "Unfortunately, that doesn't account for the baked goods she ate or ruined in her quest to steal from me."

Hell. "How much?" He reached for the wallet in his pocket.

Lia looked from him to Sammy and back again, still considering, calculating. He didn't know what that was, and he wanted to get out of here more than he wanted to figure it out.

"I don't want your money," she said firmly. Lia's gaze moved back to Sammy. "A couple weeks' work should pay it back. You're over fourteen, aren't you, kid?"

"I'm *sixteen*."

"She's fifteen," Gard muttered irritably. "And has school. She might be currently masquerading as brainless, but she's actually got a tough course load. I don't like the idea of her working on top of it. She's got to keep her grades up. I'll pay you back for the baked goods."

"Attentive uncle, are we?"

Gard liked to think he was an easy-going guy. But he also had a line he didn't let people cross. Usually, they were criminals trying to find a breaking point.

But Lia Blair sure found his quick.

She must have realized it, because her own disruptive smirk—not unlike Sammy's—melted off her face. "Weekends are my busy days and when I need help," she said in her usual no-nonsense manner. "Six to noon, Saturday and Sunday. Three weeks of that should clear up this little… misunderstanding. And it still gives her time to do all her schoolwork."

"Six in the *morning*?" Sammy squeaked.

Which settled it for Gard. Besides, if she was here, she couldn't go sneaking off, could she? Maybe she'd cause trouble *here*, but that was going to be Lia Blair's problem. "Start this Saturday?"

Lia had a lot of problems with Corporal Fairhurst. First, the fancy-pants name. Second, the fact he was a cop. Third…

God, he was hot. Tall, broad shouldered. She was sure the whole uniform getup added to the fact he looked big and intimidating, but she had a sneaking suspicion even in plain clothes he'd look big and intimidating.

And she knew she had issues, because yeah, she liked that. She would have said she didn't like short hair on guys, because it gave off that cop/military/authoritative vibe she was most assuredly *not* going for in her life.

He made it work. Then there were the eyes. A piercing, startling blue. And he had that whole *cop* distance thing down to an art, but there was a lot more going on in his eyes. Including a very clear concern over his niece.

He'd questioned her back when Albennie had been kidnapped. He'd been courteous and had a fairly good bedside manner for a cop, but still… *Cops.* She didn't trust them.

"I *hate* you," the girl seethed, then stalked out of the bakery.

Corporal Fairhurst scrubbed a palm over his jaw, let out a long sigh as his eyes followed the storming Sammy out of the bakery. But he didn't immediately follow. Lia watched him try to get a handle on his temper, and a lot of other more complex emotions going on in there.

She didn't *want* to feel a little soft around the edges, because he clearly didn't know what to do about his teenage niece but wanted to. She wanted to think of him like every other cop she'd dealt with when she'd been Sammy's age. Brutal and cruel.

Gard sighed. "I'm sorry about this. She'll be here Saturday. I'll make sure of it, but… She didn't really steal enough baked goods to necessitate three weekends of work, did she?"

Lia hesitated. She didn't owe him the truth, but he seemed to know it anyway. "No, she didn't. But if you give me three weekends, I think I can give her some…direction."

"And what do you care about a fifteen-year-old stranger's direction?" he asked, those eyes right on her and doing very uncomfortable things to her equilibrium—something she prided herself on and had all her life.

She couldn't say it was none of his business since he was clearly in charge of said niece in some capacity. "Let's just say I was once a fifteen-year-old girl lacking direction myself."

He studied her, like he could see all the *runaway teen* on her. She didn't like that at *all*.

"Her mom, my sister, has…problems. Her dad was never in the picture. Things have actually been good the past three years. Stable. But my sister…lit out again. It's a really delicate time. She's not a bad kid," he said, so earnestly it was hard not to believe him. "She's…had it bad, and sometimes she acts out because of it."

"I understand that," Lia said. Lia didn't like to think about her teenage years. What had landed her here in Hope Town. But she saw it all on Sammy, and she *had* made the job offer because she wanted to help. "We'll take good care of her, Corporal."

"Call me Gard."

"I'd rather not."

Something in him changed then. Lightened. Flipped. *Something.* Like he'd moved from trying to figure his niece out, to trying to figure *her* out. "You ever going to tell me why you don't like me?"

She crossed her arms over her chest, looked up at him. She shrugged, uncomfortable with how obvious she was. "I don't like cops."

"You like Campbell just fine."

"Royal is an exception only because he makes Franny happy, and Franny is my friend."

"So all I have to do is make one of your friends happy for you to like me?" He flashed a grin. Charming. Damn, it was charming, but he must know it. "Give me a list."

She wanted to smile. She fought it back. "Goodbye, Corporal."

Chapter Three

Gard had caught up with Sammy halfway down Main Street. She didn't argue with him when he told her to get in his patrol car, but that hadn't made his choices any easier.

He'd had to think fast to figure out what to do with her when he had two hours left on his shift. Luckily, one of his former trainees was working the zone his house was in, so he'd asked if he could switch on account of a family emergency.

Gard drove Sammy back to his house, half listening to his radio for a call and half wondering what the hell he was going to do if he got one.

Once he'd arrived at his house, he'd told Sammy to go inside and stay put. He wouldn't lecture her until he was technically off duty. She'd slammed out of his patrol car and into the house, while he'd stayed parked out front, praying he didn't get any calls he had to respond to.

Luck was in his favor—at least in this teeny, tiny part of his life, and he was able to clock out and radio off without having to leave his post.

He approached the house, wincing at the sound of music thumping from inside. He couldn't wait to hear the complaints from his neighbors. Especially since he worked with the detective who lived next door. Hart was a decent guy, and actually…

Gard looked over at the house. Maybe Hart could look into Dani's disappearance. It wouldn't be the first time Gard had asked someone at Bent County for help, but he tended to ask the same person so he didn't have to explain this to someone else.

So tomorrow, maybe he'd go talk to Laurel. She was the lead detective in Bent County these days, and she was familiar with Dani's issues.

Gard knew better, but it was always a *possibility* Dani hadn't caused her own trouble.

And when has that ever been true? Irritated with himself, he stepped inside. He went straight to the guest room where Sammy was sprawled out on the bed, nose in her phone. He figured the music thumping out of an external speaker was originating from the laptop on her desk, so he went over and flipped it closed.

Blessed silence followed. Sammy sent him one disgusted look, then went back to playing on her phone. She said nothing. Offered no apologies or excuses. Just haughty indifference.

Because she expected him to yell, lecture, punish. He wanted to—and probably should—but since she was expecting it, he started somewhere else. He couldn't let her off the hook completely, but he could…work his way around to the hook.

"Has your mom called? Texted?"

Her eyebrows drew together, unable to hide her confusion at him not approaching the subject of her *stealing.* "No."

Dani was a lot of things, but even when she was messed up, she communicated with her daughter. *You're grasping at straws.* Yeah, he was, but he couldn't stop himself. "Take me through her leaving again."

Sammy rolled onto her stomach, looking at her phone, not him. "Look, I know you want this to be different or whatever. But it's not. It's the same thing every time. She's gone. I'm screwed."

Gard knew Sammy was right. That kernel of concern that something had happened to Dani was… Well, it was never right. It was always…not wishful thinking exactly—because he didn't wish anything bad on his sister. He just wanted her to be making better choices, and she never was.

"Come on. You're helping make dinner."

She said nothing. She didn't move. She just kept looking at her phone, her thumbs moving over the screen at a rapid pace.

"Sammy."

"Not hungry," she said, not bothering to look up.

"Have you eaten anything since lunch?"

She shrugged.

He would *not* turn into his father—cold and intimidating and threatening, but man, he could feel that welling up inside of him. It left him feeling a little sick to his stomach.

But she *did* need to eat, and *God*, he hated cell phones. So he moved closer to the bed and she finally looked up at him. He took the momentary distraction to pluck the phone from her hands.

She shrieked.

"You want it back for school tomorrow? You're helping make and clean up after dinner." Then he simply walked out of the room. Calm. Direct. No yelling. No threats.

Maybe it wasn't the best move—hell, how was he supposed to know how to be a parent? But it wasn't yelling. It wasn't the silent treatment. He wouldn't withdraw love or support just because she was acting out and pissing him off.

He was *evolved.*

He went into his room and put the cell phone in the safe with his gun. He changed out of his uniform and into sweats. When he went out to the kitchen, he was surprised to find Sammy was there rather than pouting in her room with the door locked.

She gave him a cool once-over. "I don't even need my phone," she said, nose in the air. "Technological dependency is a scourge."

He did not say what he wanted—that she sure did an amazing impression of technological dependency—he just pretended he agreed. He opened the fridge and tried to think of something to make.

He tended to lean toward frozen dinners, sandwiches, or something canned, so he was a little at a loss staring at the contents of his fridge. "Well…" At least a sandwich could have a few different food groups. Maybe he could heat up a can of soup with them and—

"I'll make spaghetti," Sammy said, sounding disgusted with him. Or maybe just life.

"I can do it."

She gave him a little shove away from the refrigerator. "No, you'll put extra salt in the sauce and make it gross. I'll do it."

He opened his mouth to argue some more. She was in a lot of trouble, and her making dinner certainly didn't get her out of it, and he didn't feel right having someone else make him a meal. Not these days.

"I like it," she muttered. "Let me do it."

Since she muttered the *I like it* part, he figured she wasn't lying. "All right. You cook. I'll clean."

She perked up a little at that, surprising Gard. He tried to keep up with what she liked, but he hadn't heard anything about a desire to spend time in the kitchen. Still, he watched her work. She knew her way around his kitchen even though she'd never cooked here before—likely because he'd organized Dani's kitchen in the apartment in Fairmont the same way he did his.

Gard sat down at the table, keeping an eye on her over the counter that separated kitchen from dining room. As he watched her put everything together, he realized…she *was* enjoying herself. She was concentrating, cutting up tomatoes and inspecting his array of spices. She didn't have that permanent teenage-rebellion scowl on her face as she poured dry pasta into boiling water and stirred whatever sauce concoction she was making.

When it was all done, she even made up two plates—complete with toasted bread slathered in butter. She brought them to the table.

"Are you really going to make me go to work at *six in the morning* on a *weekend*?" she asked, sliding the plate in front of him. "That's like…child abuse."

Since *she* brought it up, he figured it was fair game now. "How about this? Don't steal. You won't earn yourself a job." And him the complication of having to finagle some afternoons off so he could pick her up from the bakery. He tended to work most weekends since he didn't have a wife or kids to see, and most of his friends were first responders working nontraditional hours.

She shrugged, sliding into the seat across from him. "It's fun."

He didn't groan or grimace or close his eyes in quiet supplication to some higher power to *help him survive this*. He tried to remain even-keeled and unimpressed. No matter how he felt about the idea of stealing being *fun*.

"Well, it's not going to be fun when you don't have a nice bakery owner to bail you out and I have no choice but to have someone I work with actually arrest you."

"It'd just be juvie."

Gard rolled his eyes. She didn't have a damn clue, but she certainly thought she did. *Teenagers.* "You want to stay out of the system, Sammy? Follow the rules." He took a bite of the plate of food she'd put in front of him, chewed thoughtfully, then narrowed his eyes at her. "Hey, this is really good. What did you do to it?"

He watched as she tried to fight her pleasure over the compliment. "It's just spaghetti."

"Maybe, but that's not just generic brand sauce from a jar. Believe me, I know."

"I just doctored it up a little bit."

"It's amazing. Be careful. I could get used to this."

She ducked her head, clearly trying to hide a smile. Which made him feel a bit like he'd won the lottery—a very strange, warped lottery, but a win nonetheless.

He didn't bring up the stealing again. He asked about school. About her schedule. They talked about getting her driver's permit. He had a lot of realities to figure out now that he suddenly had a fifteen-year-old to take care of. In some ways, that was easier than when she'd been a baby or a toddler, but it still required a lot of reconfiguring his life.

But he'd never want her to know just how much effort it was, because he'd do it a million times if it kept her safe.

They did not talk about Dani. They did not talk about her decidedly *not* going to this Model UN meeting and instead heading to Hope Town to *steal*.

Gard knew that was probably a failure on his part, but

he just couldn't bring himself to ruin the ease of this dinner with the negative subject of her…breaking the *law*.

When Sammy got up to take her plate to the sink, he stopped her. "Nope. I'm on cleanup duty."

Sammy considered him, then shrugged and put her plate back down. "'Kay."

"You got homework?"

She rolled her eyes. "Yes."

"Then get on it."

"Mom never asks if I have homework."

"That's because your mom didn't graduate high school. You plan on following in those footsteps?"

She wrinkled her nose, regarded him with serious blue eyes. "Were you really going to go to law school?"

Gard blinked in surprise. "She told you that?"

"Yeah. She was worrying about money, and I said she should just ask you for some."

"When was this?" Gard asked, too quick he knew. Too cop-like, because Sammy's expression went guarded.

Sammy shrugged. "Few months ago. She said you'd already given up enough for us, and she wasn't coming to you for more money, and when I asked what *that* meant, she said law school and being rich and important like her dad."

Gard frowned. Dani had been working at a restaurant in Fairmont the past two years. She'd claimed she was making enough. She was supposed to ask him if she needed help. *He* didn't have a kid to support. He had the money, and he wanted to help.

Why hadn't she just asked him? But since Dani wasn't here, he couldn't lecture her about asking for help. He had to deal with the story she'd told Sammy. Did Dani believe all that BS? Did she really not understand?

Sammy would. He'd make sure of it. He looked right at

her and delivered a speech he'd given Dani too many times to count. More repeating patterns he couldn't seem to stop.

"I didn't give up law school *for* you guys. I gave up law school because the way my parents treated your mom when she was struggling was a wake-up call. I didn't want to follow the path they'd set for me—being a lawyer and being cruel like them. I wanted to follow my own path. So I didn't go to law school. It was no great sacrifice. It was a choice I made. Don't let her ever tell you otherwise."

Sammy watched him carefully, but he couldn't read what was behind all that careful survey. "But you have sacrificed for us, even if you didn't sacrifice that."

He wanted to lie to her, but he figured she'd see right through that. "That's what family should do, Sam. When it matters."

She looked down at her now-empty plate.

"Sammy." There were so many things he wanted to say. He struggled to find the words to express what he felt, what she needed to know. Gard and Dani had grown up in a house of hard words. Or no words. Criticism and high expectations. Icy silences, withdrawn support. No one spoke of *love*, just respect and failing to meet expectations. They might have had all the material things in life, but they hadn't had anything deeper, anything soft.

Gard still struggled with expressing those softer things, but if he'd learned anything in the years of trying to deal with Dani's addiction, Sammy growing up with just him and Dani as support, it was that he didn't want words left unsaid just because he was afraid to be uncomfortable or vulnerable.

And he'd use whatever words, whatever feelings, whatever soft, sharp truths to make sure Sammy knew that she was loved, cared for. That she was *important*. He couldn't make her choices for her, or Dani's, but he could do that.

"I know her doing this again hurts. It hurts me too. I love her, and I'd do anything to fix this for her. For you."

Sammy shoved away from the table. "I'm going to do my homework."

But Gard was faster, and he blocked her path to the room. She stood there, gaze on the floor, shoulders hunched and rounded forward as if she could protect herself from the soft words.

He pulled her into a hug, squeezed her tight. "It would be worth any sacrifice, because you both matter," he said softly.

She didn't pull away, but she did look up then, tears in her eyes. "I thought it was enough this time. I really believed…she wouldn't go back this time."

Gard had to swallow against his own tight throat as his heart cracked in two—not the first time Dani had done that to him. Hopefully not the last because he needed her to come back, even if she broke his heart a million more times. "Me too, baby. Me too."

"So, we're hiring criminals now?"

Lia didn't spare Albennie a glance. Even though she was breaking the no-talking-the-first-hour-at-the-bakery rule. "She's fifteen."

"Fifteen-year-olds can still be criminals."

Since Lia knew that from experience, she could hardly argue with Albennie. "We'll have her do prep. Wash dishes. Keep her in the kitchen and away from the till. It'll be fine."

"You're too softhearted."

Lia snorted. Not something she'd ever been accused of. Except from Albennie. Who, in fairness, probably knew her better than anybody. So maybe she should be a little worried about that soft heart.

The bell on the door tinkled, so they moved out of the kitchen to the main area. Sammy stepped in first, looking just as surly as she had the day she'd played thief. Gard was dressed in his uniform behind her.

"God, he's hot," Albennie said quietly, fanning herself with a dishcloth.

"You say that about every cop who walks in here," Lia said irritably, because he *was* hot and she didn't want him to be. Bad enough when he was a random figure on the periphery of her social life. Worse when she was starting to see the man behind the uniform.

An uncle who cared about his teenage charge, who was that hot, and now far more in her orbit was a recipe for disaster.

Lia snatched the dishcloth out of Albennie's hands and stepped forward with a smile that had to have looked more like a grimace thanks to Albennie's words. "Morning, guys."

"Good morning," Gard greeted cheerfully.

Sammy only grunted. Which Lia supposed was the reason behind Gard's cheer.

"Sammy, this is Albennie," Lia said. "She's going to show you your first exciting job of the morning. Measuring out ingredients."

"Whatever," Sammy muttered.

Albennie sent Lia a look, but Lia ignored the clear disapproval in it. Albennie was all talk anyway. She'd be nice and patient with Sammy, because that was who Albennie was under that tough outer shell.

A pair of softhearted women was what they were. *Recipe for absolute disaster.*

"Follow me, Sammy," Albennie said, waving Sammy back into the kitchen.

Since Gard was still standing there, Lia stayed put. "You want a cup of coffee? To go," she clarified quickly.

His mouth curved a little, like he knew that little tack on was because he made her…nervous. *Ugh.*

"No. Thanks." His expression sobered. "Listen, I don't suppose there's any way you could keep her around until three?"

Lia frowned at him, and she had to actually tilt her head up a little. She was tall for a woman, so she wasn't used to having to look up at people too often, but he was *tall.*

And built.

Not the point of anything right now. "You want me to babysit? I thought you took the afternoon off to come by and pick her up." He'd told her that when he'd called the bakery yesterday to confirm their plans.

"You're the one who insisted she work here. Look…" There was something in his eyes then. Expression carefully blank, but something in those deep blue depths. She couldn't have put a label on it, but it had all that *soft* bubbling up.

Oh, she was in some trouble.

Gard leaned forward, lowered his voice, and the fact her stomach jittered in ways it should *not* only verified trouble was in the offing.

"I just have to…" He trailed off like he wasn't quite sure how much to give away. "I can't trust Sammy on her own right now, and I have to… I have to make sure Sammy's mom isn't in more trouble than usual. I know you don't owe her or me a damn thing, but you're the one sticking your nose in and giving her a job. So, I figure this can't be asking too much. Put her to work."

"And if she wreaks havoc?"

Gard's mouth quirked up on one side, a lot like he expected Sammy to do exactly that. "I'll owe you one."

How he made that seem…serious but also kind of flirty—which she was *not* responding to—Lia wasn't about to parse.

Lia crossed her arms over her chest and sighed gustily. "Fine."

"Thanks. Really. I'll owe you one anyway." He glanced beyond the counter where Albennie had taken Sammy. Then that direct, blue gaze was back on Lia. "She's a good kid. I know I'm biased, but she *is*. She deserves some kind of break, and I don't know how to give her one."

That soft heart Albennie accused her of having fluttered, because it was just so clear he *cared*. And that was not something Lia had seen very much of. Particularly from the male species—in and out of a uniform.

"I'll see what I can do."

Chapter Four

Gard's first stop after he dropped Sammy off in Hope Town was to head to the sheriff's department for roll call. Then he'd work half his shift before taking off at noon like he'd originally planned. Because he hadn't canceled his afternoon off. He was going on a little recon mission.

Sure, Dani had likely fallen off the wagon, so to speak. Maybe she was hiding out because she was embarrassed. Maybe she was just "enjoying life" as she'd so often put it in the past. And maybe, he should just *let her*, but he couldn't. He had to know for sure, then make a decision with all the pertinent facts. Because Sammy needed a *legal* guardian if Dani wasn't going to be around to be that.

At times, Gard had been that, so he knew what steps to take, but if this was just a little one-off, just a little…mistake on Dani's part… He had to know for sure before he moved forward.

So, he was going to look into it. Just try to figure out where she might have gone. Even if it was to get high and ruin her life, *again*, at least he'd know she wasn't just… dead in a ditch. Gone forever. Lost forever.

He shook off the worst-case scenarios. He saw plenty in his job, so he could hardly pretend they didn't exist, but he didn't need to reimagine old events in his professional life with his sister's face on the victims.

On his way out of the building, he happened to pass by the detective bureau's office and caught sight of Laurel sitting at her desk. The other two detectives, including his neighbor Hart, were not in there with her.

He shouldn't do it. He should let this be, handle it himself if he was going to be pathetic, but… He poked his head in her office. "Detective. You got a minute?"

"Sure, Fairhurst. Come on in."

When he stepped in and closed the door behind him, she raised an eyebrow. Then offered a sad smile. "Your sister?"

"Yeah." The first time Dani had dropped Sammy off with him and disappeared, he'd been at his first police job in Dubois. He'd gone to his parents for help.

They'd started talking about having Sammy taken away from Dani and never letting Dani have *any* access to her ever again.

Gard still felt guilty about that—how close he'd come to ruining Dani's *and* Sammy's lives. Because Gard knew that his parents would have *never* shown Sammy an ounce of love.

Luckily, his parents hadn't wanted to explain taking care of their granddaughter to their important friends, so Gard had weaseled out of that plan. And he'd vowed never to go back to his parents for help again. In fact, he hadn't spoken to them since.

In the end, Dani had shown up just three days later, apologetic and ready to get help—the very first time she'd ever admitted she had a problem. Gard had been hopeful.

She'd made it two years that time. He'd been at Bent County the second time Dani had dropped Sammy off and lit out. Gard hadn't asked for help—too burned by his parents. He'd just done his level best to take care of Sammy and do his job.

When Dani had come back after a week, Gard had decided it was time to get proactive. Not just rehab—family therapy, adding him as a legal guardian of Sammy, and the three of them moving in together.

That had lasted six years. Dani had disappeared twice in that time. The first time Gard had tried to handle everything himself, but Sammy had been old enough to really get it and he'd been at his wit's end, enough to say something in passing to fellow deputy Laurel Delaney—she hadn't been married or a detective yet at that time.

Without judgment—or involving any DFS authorities—Laurel had tracked down Dani and given him the information. So, the second time it had happened, he'd gone to her again. She'd been a detective and Delaney-*Carson* by that time, but she'd done the same thing. Tracked Dani down to some flophouse up in Hardy.

Gard had promised himself that time, he wouldn't drag anyone else into things. The next time Dani screwed up, he was done. He'd been young and naive and hadn't understood child development at all—but now he'd been to therapy, he'd read the books, and he understood that Dani's behavior was likely to impact Sammy as negatively as his own parents' cruelty had.

But here he was. Still trying to protect Dani.

Because ever since then, she'd slowly rebuilt her life. The first year had been iffy, and included some setbacks, but she hadn't disappeared anymore. The second year had been good for all of them. She'd even been the one to come to *him* and said he needed to move out, so she didn't have a safety net. So she could prove to all of them she was done falling back.

That had started really good years. Dani surviving, staying put, staying clean. Sammy thriving—she was so smart and doing so well in school, happy and involved and *loved*.

Gard had stepped back farther and farther, until their relationship had begun to feel normal instead of *codependent*.

Of course, he'd always be Dani's safety net, and Sammy's for that matter. No matter what he told himself, he couldn't let that go.

Case in point. This discussion he was having with Laurel.

"She could lose custody if I file a missing persons, so I don't want to go that route yet, but she's cut off communication with Sammy and that isn't like her." He was really holding on to that even though experience told him nothing was ever really different.

Laurel asked the relevant questions—when had Sammy last seen her and where. What did he think might have happened. What did he want Laurel to look into.

"I'll poke around," Laurel agreed. "Off the record."

"You know I appreciate it."

"Any time, Corporal."

Gard knew Laurel meant it. She'd never once acted put out or given him a lecture about working within the system. Still, it left him feeling…heavy with guilt that he couldn't figure this out himself. That he couldn't *solve* any of these problems like he wanted to.

So he went through the morning with that heavy weight on his shoulders, and it certainly didn't lift at noon when he radioed off duty, went home, and changed into plainclothes, switched out his county-issued gun for his personal one

He *had* planned to pick up Sammy, not have her spend extra hours at the bakery, but… It just didn't sit right, and he knew his gut was all sorts of messed up when it came to his sister and her choices, but he'd made a deal with himself: If she contacted him or Sammy, he'd back off.

Until she did, he got to look for her. And since he couldn't do it on the county's time, he'd do it on his own.

First, he went to Dani and Sammy's apartment in Fairmont. He had a key, so he let himself in. He didn't know what he was looking for. Some kind of clue of where Dani's head was at. What Sammy had said at dinner the other night still stuck with him. That Dani had been worried about money.

She *should* have asked him, and he couldn't understand why she didn't. In the past, she'd never had any problem asking him for money. Though that was usually when she was using.

Just another tick in the column of *abnormal*. Because Dani had a *pattern*, damn it. People didn't just deviate from fifteen-plus-year patterns without a big reason.

Like right now? He was reverting to *his* pattern. Invading Dani's privacy by snooping through her apartment. Looking for some miraculous reason this was *different* than every other time.

The place was clean, if cluttered. There were a few dishes in the sink, an empty soda can on the living room end table. When he eased into Dani's room, the real mess exploded. Clothes everywhere. Used glasses on just about every surface, along with makeup and jewelry. Not surprising. She claimed organization and cleaning gave her PTSD, and maybe it did. God knew they'd been expected to be military neat and orderly growing up. But Dani made an effort to keep her messy tendency in check in common spaces…for Sammy.

She so desperately wanted to be a good mom. She tried

so damn hard. It was why he'd never been able to give up on her.

Gard sighed heavily, tried to blow out all his conflicting feelings with it. This was just an investigation. Just looking for facts, not to dredge up all his feelings of loss, inadequacy, and regret.

Her laptop was on her nightstand, still plugged into the wall. He unplugged it, made a mental note to unplug any other unnecessary appliances before he left since he didn't know when anyone would be back.

He knew her passwords to everything, because she used the same one or a variation of it for everything. Because he'd had to at certain points in their lives, to help Sammy.

S@mmy58. Because Sammy had been born May 8. So he typed it in to log into her computer ignoring any conflicting feelings he didn't have time for.

He'd deal with those later, when Dani was found and back and *okay*.

The notes app was front and center, with an address typed out. There was no town name or zip code, but since Gard had patrolled every inch of Bent County, he knew 7653 Dry Road was out near Wilde.

He copied and pasted the address into the internet browser. The picture that came up was of a farmhouse that looked a little worse for the wear.

Hmm.

Well, what could it hurt? If it was a dead end, he'd go pick up Sammy a little early. And if it was something else…

Well, he'd deal with that.

Wilde was a good forty-five minute drive from Fairmont, and he knew he couldn't spend much time at the address and get to Hope Town in time to pick up Sammy by the promised three o'clock.

He'd just do a drive-by. See if he could glean any clues. It didn't make sense Dani was doing anything out in Wilde. If it was just about drugs, Dani surely could have got them in Fairmont.

Wishful thinking, Fairhurst.

So he drove, maybe sped a little, trying not to let his thoughts speed too as he turned onto Dry Road. On one side of the road, rows of corn grew in tall, neat rows. On the other side, he passed gravel driveways marked with numbers spread pretty far apart.

He saw 7651, a gravel drive without a marking, and then 7655, so he backtracked to the unmarked drive and turned onto the gravel. The house wasn't far back off the road. It looked a lot worse in person than it had on its picture. One front window was cracked beyond repair, a window on the second floor was boarded up. The porch sagged—and there were no stairs up to it, just a pile of warped boards where stairs would have once been.

There were no cars, but plenty of junk in the front yard. Rusted-out bikes and tools and other unidentifiable things. Gard eyed the house. It looked pretty abandoned.

He should leave it at that.

Instead, he parked on the scrubby lawn and got out of the car. He kept one hand on his holster as he moved quietly and carefully toward the front door. It looked like there *had* been a storm door at one point, but it had fallen off—or been ripped off—its hinges and tossed into the corner of the porch. The heavy wood door to the house was slightly ajar.

Trying to avoid creaking spots, Gard climbed onto the porch, slow, steady, stealthy. He thought he heard…voices coming from inside the house.

Calm from years of experience in police work and approaching possibly dangerous scenarios, he crept closer to the door. If he could get close enough without making noise on this crumbling porch, maybe he could hear what was being said. It sounded like low voices, men, but maybe Dani was in there. Maybe this really was a clue. Maybe…

He leaned forward, desperate to hear something. And it was that desperation that got him in trouble. He knew better, always knew better when it came to work.

But Dani was a whole other story.

So when the door flew open, he wasn't ready for it, and it crashed right into his face. Pain bloomed from his nose as he jerked back, stumbled, but managed to keep his footing.

Someone ran out of the door, leaping off the porch like a bat out of hell. Gard ignored the throbbing pain echoing through his skull and the feel of liquid oozing out of his nose and grabbed for his gun.

"Bent—" Hell, he wasn't on duty, so he could hardly invoke Bent County. But he did have a gun. "Stop!"

The guy, of course, did not stop. And Gard could hardly shoot at him—especially when the man leaped into the cornfield across the street and disappeared. Maybe if Gard was on duty, he'd have ventured into the tall corn and tried to find the guy, but that hardly seemed smart without backup.

He glanced back at the house, wiping the blood dripping over his mouth with the back of his hand. The door was wide open, thanks to the runaway. Gard had his gun in his hand. What was the harm in looking around?

Who had this guy been talking to? It had to be somebody. He held his gun out in front of him and crept inside. Quickly and thoroughly, he went through the entire house, but it was completely empty of people.

The guy must have been talking to himself, or maybe on the phone, which made sense, because while the house was empty of *people*, there was plenty of evidence of drugs. The kind of evidence that certainly wasn't as old as the rest of the abandoned items in and around the house.

Damn it all to hell.

LIA WAS DESPERATELY trying to think of anything else for Sammy to do, but it was well after three now and there was no sign of Gard. Why the hell had she gotten involved in this mess of a situation? Was she now going to be in charge of a teenager while Gard Fairhurst gallivanted around doing who knew what?

Not that Sammy was a problem. She'd been a little sloppy with measuring ingredients. She had not been at *all* thorough with cleaning, but she'd shown an interest in the actual food prep. Lia couldn't let her jump on only the things she liked, but she figured if she could get the girl interested in learning how to make at least one bakery item, Lia could hold it over her head like a bribe to get her to do the less fun parts.

Albennie had headed home for the day. Lia had even closed up the store. Should she call Gard? He'd left his cell phone number. Maybe a text. A casual *Hey, you remember you have a niece to pick up, right?*

But it made her nervous. Because he'd *seemed* like he was very dedicated to Sammy. And he definitely didn't strike her as flighty—but maybe she'd been fooled by piercing blue eyes and an unfairly handsome face.

Wouldn't that just figure?

Her bakery phone rang, causing her to jump. It was after hours, but she had a feeling she knew who the caller would be. "Hope Town Bakery."

"Hey, Lia, it's Gard. Um. I have another favor to ask of you."

"You're just full of them," she muttered irritably, but he sounded…weird. Not that she had any great insight into what Gard Fairhurst sounded like over the phone. Just that there was something…nasally and muffled about him.

"I'm running late, so I was wondering… Look, it's a lot to ask, but do you think you could meet me at my place and drop Sammy off for me? The bakery is closed, right?"

"Yeah, it's closed. Look, Corporal—"

"I just had a little…accident. Had to get patched up at the hospital in Fairmont. No big deal, but—"

Hospital. That was serious. And almost made her feel bad for thinking the worst of him. "What kind of accident?"

He was silent for a moment. A hesitation. "Broke my nose is all. Nothing serious. Not the first time even."

He'd *broken* his nose—probably on duty. And was being all nonchalant about it. Maybe he'd deserved it. Lia wouldn't have minded popping a few cops in the nose given a chance.

Lia slid a glance at Sammy, who was staring at her. What was she going to do—tell the guy in the hospital *no* while his niece stared at her?

"Yeah, I'll drive her."

"Okay, I'm heading out now. If you guys leave now too, we should get there about the same time."

"Sure. Yeah. See you in a bit." She hung up the phone and stared at it. Now she was driving this problem child home? All because she couldn't just accept the stolen money being repaid. *Creating your own trouble, Lia.*

"What was that?" Sammy demanded.

"Your uncle got…held up." Lia didn't know why she was lying for him, but she didn't really want to be the one who broke it to the girl that her uncle was hurt. "I'm going to drive you to his place. You got an address?"

"Yeah, but…" Sammy trailed off, then shook her head. "Whatever."

"We're going to have to walk over to my house and get my car, so follow me."

Sammy said nothing but followed Lia out of the back of the bakery. She waited, nose stuck to phone screen, while Lia locked the door and engaged the alarm. Even though Sammy never looked up from the phone screen, she unerringly followed Lia down the side street to her house.

Lia walked up to her car, unlocked it manually because her key fob had been broken for approximately three years.

"Hop on in," she said to Sammy.

Sammy looked at the car in disgust. "Will this make it *to* Bent?"

"Sure." Maybe it wasn't anything to look at. Maybe it burned oil here and there. Maybe it was older than Sammy herself, but Lia had bought this car with her own money. So Lia loved it.

She slid into the driver's seat and then followed Sammy's somewhat distracted directions to the small town of Bent, and a quaint little neighborhood right off the main drag.

"This one," Sammy said, pointing to a pretty brick one-story.

Gard Fairhurst's house was nothing that Lia would have imagined. It didn't scream *single male cop lives here*, except for the patrol car sitting in the driveway. The sweet little brick ranch house on the main drag of Bent seemed more suited for a family. Sure, he didn't have the pretty landscaping his neighbor did, but the yard was neat. His windows looked clean.

Lia had a feeling this incongruous house had to do with the girl sitting in her passenger seat. She pulled her car into

Park on the curb just as a truck pulled into the drive next to the patrol car.

Gard immediately got out and skirted the truck. He had a splint on his nose—so he hadn't been making anything up. There was an awful lot of blood on his T-shirt.

Something about *that* had Lia getting out of her car at the same time as Sammy. Moving toward him with the strange thought she should…do something about it.

"Thanks for driving her," Gard offered as Sammy rushed up to him.

"What happened?" Sammy demanded.

"It's nothing. I'm fine." He smiled down at Sammy, but between the splint on his nose and the clear pain in his eyes, it didn't look like a happy smile. He slung an arm over her shoulders, but clearly Sammy wasn't happy with the brush-off.

"What happened?" she said again, more seriously this time.

"Door to the nose, accidentally. I think. Wasn't expecting it, obviously. It's broken. It'll heal."

Sammy was staring at the blood on his shirt, and Lia couldn't help but do the same. It was *a lot* of blood.

"Thanks, Lia. Really. I owe—"

"Why did a door hit your face?" Sammy demanded, but her voice was squeaky, and Lia realized she was crying about the same time Gard did.

He squeezed her to his side. "Hey. *Hey.* It's nothing. Really. I've had way worse."

Which was not the thing to say, because Sammy started crying even harder.

Gard looked up at Lia helplessly. She sure as hell didn't know what to do though. She was tempted to turn and run—get in her car and *go.* Except her feet seem rooted to the spot, at the end of his driveway, looking at the blood on his shirt and the protective arm around his niece.

"You're not in your uniform," Sammy said, her voice squeaky. She sniffled as she pulled back from where she'd buried her head in his chest. She looked up at him—tears were all over her cheeks but there was something closer to accusation in her eyes. "You weren't at work?"

Gard opened his mouth, but no words came out, and everything about Sammy's demeanor changed. She stepped out from his arm, her expression mutinous.

"You were looking for Mom."

Lia noted the girl didn't sound happy about that. And Gard looked *guilty* as hell.

"Just…poking around."

"Poking around and getting *hurt*," Sammy replied, backing away from him. "She's using. She left. Just let it be." Sammy whirled away, stormed inside, slammed the door behind her so it echoed into the quiet afternoon.

Lia felt frozen in place. This was…so none of her business. Why was she even here? "I, um, should go."

"Yeah, look. I really appreciate it." But he sounded so damn defeated.

Soft heart. Soft heart. Soft heart.

"She's just upset you're hurt."

He sighed, glancing at the house. "Maybe, but she's got every right to be pissed at me too. Dani…she's struggled with substance abuse since she was Sammy's age. These disappearing acts have been going on Sammy's whole life. The family therapist has told me time and time again it's not my job, or Sammy's job, to fix it."

But he wanted to. That much was written all over him.

And in spite of herself, or maybe because of herself and

all the people she'd known and lost to various bad decisions, she stuck her nose into this mess even further.

"Any time you need something for her to do, I'm happy to help. I can even have her help with inventory after hours or stuff like that. Doesn't just have to be weekends."

He studied her for a minute, an intense and uncomfortable study. She wanted to call it a *cop* look, but it wasn't about cop things. It was about Sammy.

"That's really kind, and I appreciate the offer, I do. But you don't owe us anything."

No, she didn't. Not even an explanation, but here it came anyway. "Sometimes…you want to be the person you needed as a kid for someone else."

His gaze held hers, serious. "Yeah, sometimes you do."

The moment held. Just the two of them looking at each other—and he looked ridiculous with that metal splint on his face, but it didn't seem to dilute all that piercing blue. Or the effect it had on her insides and their incessant *fluttering* when he was around.

She looked away. Pulled her phone out of her pocket and pulled up her contact information. She had to take a few steps forward to be close enough to hold it out to him.

"Here's my phone number. My cell, not the bakery."

He pulled out his own phone, poked at his screen a few times. "Here, can you put it in for me? This hurts like hell."

Soft heart. Soft heart. Soft heart. She took his phone wordlessly, added herself as a new contact, then handed the phone back. "I'll see you tomorrow…Gard."

His mouth quirked to one side, no doubt that she'd finally used his first name, then he kind of winced, no doubt because his nose hurt. "See you tomorrow, Lia."

Chapter Five

A little over a week passed quickly and surprisingly uneventfully—Gard got the splint off his nose and mostly healed up. He stopped looking for Dani, because if she had the address of a drug house on her computer, it was clear she'd just fallen back into old patterns.

It hurt, and he still *wanted* to track her down, still worried she hadn't contacted Sammy, but he couldn't screw up his own life—or, more importantly, Sammy's—to do it. Sammy getting so upset about his nose and him looking for Dani was a harsh reminder that he was all she had now, and he had to act accordingly.

Laurel would keep an eye out and an ear to the ground and let him know if she heard anything about Dani, but that was all Gard could allow himself. Sammy had to be his priority now.

So, he rearranged his schedule as best he could to be able to drive her where she needed to be and be around when she was home. He took her to family therapy, learned how to check her grades, tried to vet her rides that weren't him, and, in the end, he let her spend way too much time at the Hope Town Bakery.

He worked around the system a little so that on the off chance they could locate Dani, get her into some rehab, she wouldn't have ruined her shot at being in Sammy's life, but he also knew even if she came back—it was going to be Gard's responsibility to get Sammy through these last years of high school. So he didn't plan for Dani's return.

Just hoped.

Lia claimed Sammy didn't cause any trouble at the bakery and was learning how to decorate cookies like a pro. Lia claimed she was an *asset*.

Gard chose to believe her, because what else was there to do? Lia saw Sammy as some kind of…karmic chance to be the help she'd never had as a teen, so if she was lying about Sammy behaving it was about that—not covering for Sammy.

Besides, Sammy had seemed so pleased when Lia had called her an asset. Sure, she was still moody and unpredictable but working at the bakery was having a positive effect on this transition period.

Gard tried to imagine what Lia Blair had been like as a teen. To hate cops. To sympathize with a girl who would steal. What had *she* gone through?

Truth be told, he found himself thinking a little too much about Lia Blair.

If Sammy wasn't involved, he'd have probably asked her out by now. He'd wormed his way under that original dislike and distrust, he liked to think. She called him Gard now. She even smiled at him on occasion.

And he liked the challenge—because he didn't quite know what Lia Blair would say. She'd be tempted, he knew that—whatever she felt about *him* as a person, they were attracted to each other. But he was curious if she'd turn him down or take a chance.

But Sammy existed as a line he didn't want to cross. So maybe he flirted, but he didn't push it beyond that.

It was getting a little harder though. Because here he was, dropping some papers off at the sheriff's department before he went off duty, excited to get to the bakery. Where he'd chat with Lia for ten minutes or so about Sammy's progress, or sometimes he could get her off topic. The weather, the bakery, music, movies.

"Fairhurst, you got a minute?"

Gard turned from the mailboxes to see Detective Copeland Beckett striding toward him. Probably about a case, though Gard didn't know of any active investigations the detectives were handling that involved him. Still, Gard was used to answering whatever questions the detectives had about calls he might have responded to.

"Sure, what's up?"

"You know that drug house you came across off duty?"

Gard tried not to stiffen. He'd reported what he'd seen, but not why he'd been there. "Yeah."

"Is this the guy you saw run out of it?" Beckett held out a picture, grainy, black and white, clearly from some security footage.

Gard studied it—the proportions of the body, the profile of the face. "I didn't get the best look at him since he was running, but…this doesn't seem quite right."

Beckett nodded taking the picture back. "This guy is six-two, two-ten. Scar on the side of his neck."

"Yeah, definitely not the runner. He was under six feet and scrawny. Does this guy in the picture own the place or something?"

"No. Haven't been able to track down an owner, but a case I'm looking into had this guy using that address on a job application."

"No one was living there. I looked through the whole house. No signs of anything but drug use."

"Yeah, that's why I'm curious. Why use an address that's just a house full of drug paraphernalia?" Beckett shook his head. "Anyway, thanks. Just wanted to make sure we couldn't physically connect him."

"Sure. Yeah."

Beckett turned and started to walk away, but Gard followed. "Just out of curiosity, what kind of case is it?"

"The Hardy Police Department has been dealing with some reports of possible human trafficking. They've asked for some assistance, and it led us to this guy." Beckett held up the picture. "Might be nothing, just talk, but we're going to get to the bottom of it."

A little trickle of cold unease crept up his spine. But that was ridiculous. He couldn't assume Dani's disappearance was anything but what it usually was.

Except she hasn't contacted Sammy.

Beckett walked away and Gard stood there, arguing internally with himself. Maybe Dani was connected to that house somehow—drugs no doubt, but the guy he'd seen run out of it was not the guy Beckett was looking for. Thinking Dani had somehow gotten mixed up in a human trafficking ring in *Hardy* was a leap with no real evidence.

He tried to set aside the unease, but it stayed.

And no doubt would, until he looked into it himself.

At two o'clock, Albennie went home, leaving Lia and Sammy to finish up the day together. It was getting to be almost normal.

It was getting to be *nice.* The girl was sarcastic, constantly on her phone, a little self-obsessed…and funny, creative, and genuinely interested in baking. It was like whiplash every day—frustration and fascination. Wanting to help the girl. Wanting to throttle her.

Like right now, when Sammy was purposefully dawdling instead of going out to the main room and cleaning up the tables, which was always her last job of the day. A job she did *not* like and tried to avoid.

"It's two thirty," Lia said, speaking loudly to get through the screen-haze Sammy was often in.

"Yeah," Sammy agreed, not looking up from her phone. Lia could see she was watching baking videos. Which was somehow both heartwarming and *irritating* since the girl was *in a bakery* and had a job to do that *involved* baking, so maybe she could save the videos for home.

"You're supposed to be cleaning the tables, remember?"

"Yeah," Sammy agreed, swiping up to the next video. She didn't move. Clearly, she wasn't actually listening.

Trying to breathe through her frustration, Lia lost that last grip on patience. She put her fingers in her mouth and let out a piercing whistle. Then sharply said, "Sammy."

Sammy looked up, blinking in confusion. "What?" she demanded in what could only be described as teenage disgust, like Lia was overreacting when Lia wouldn't have whistled if Sammy had *listened*.

Teenagers. Natural gaslighters.

"It is time to clean the front tables," Lia said between clenched teeth.

Sammy sighed dramatically but shoved her phone into her pocket and headed for the front room. The bell on the door tinkled at the same time, so Lia followed to wait on the customer.

Sammy stopped short at the archway between the kitchen and the storefront. So abruptly Lia almost ran into her back.

"I can't go out there," Sammy hissed.

"Why not?"

"Because I know that girl."

Lia looked out at the bakery. A teenage girl had just walked in with a woman. Maybe a mother and daughter, but they didn't look much alike and were maybe a little too close in age.

"And why can't you clean up the tables while a girl you know is here?"

"Because it's embarrassing!"

"You know what else is embarrassing?"

Sammy glared at her. "You're going to say *stealing money and getting caught.*"

"Bingo, kid." But Lia was a softy, as previously established. She gave Sammy a little nudge forward. "Go take their order."

Sammy blinked at her. "You're going to let me use the cash register?"

"Go take their order. Before I change my mind. Or they do about coming here and you cost me paying customers."

Sammy practically skipped out to the counter, though some of that enthusiasm faded when the other teenage girl looked at her.

Lia watched, ready to jump in if need be. Maybe she should have let Sammy hide. Maybe this was some sort of mean girl situation.

"I can take your order," Sammy said, sounding a little shy.

"Hey, Sammy," the girl greeted with a friendly smile. She looked around the room. "You work here?"

"Yeah."

"That is so cool." She shot a look at the woman with her. "My dad said if I want a job, I have to work for *him*." She rolled her eyes.

"Yeah, playing with dogs is a real hardship," the woman muttered. "Can we get two frozen mochas and two chocolate chip muffins?"

Sammy dutifully punched the order into the tablet and then offered a total. The woman paid with card, so that was easy enough for Sammy to figure out, and Lia got started on the coffees while Sammy packaged up two muffins.

"Hey, did you understand the math homework?" the girl asked Sammy.

Lia glanced over her shoulder to see Sammy shaking her head, not quite meeting the girl's steady eye contact.

"Do you know Sarabeth Thompson?" the girl persisted.

Sammy nodded, still being uncharacteristically mute.

"We're going to meet up before school tomorrow—Sarabeth's great at math, so she was going to help me. Then we're both going to try to figure out what the heck gerunds are. Grammar makes me want to *die*."

Sammy said nothing. Lia kind of wanted to go over there and poke her into saying something. Clearly the other teen was being nice, friendly.

Luckily, the visitor just kept talking. "We're going to meet in Coach Swift's room, if you want to come by. Maybe we can all help each other. Who do you have for English?"

"Uh, Mrs. Brandt. I'm in…honors."

"Oh my God." The girl leaned over the counter with hopeful enthusiasm. "Do *you* understand gerunds?"

Sammy shrugged. "Kind of, I guess."

"Even better. Sarabeth will help us with math, and you can help us with English. Are you in bio?"

"Yeah."

"Perfect. I can help you with that. I'm in chemistry this year because I'm ahead in science. Do you have Mr. Mallory?"

Sammy nodded.

"I had him last year. Stop by if you can get to school early, okay? We'll help each other out."

If Sammy didn't agree, Lia was about to agree for her, but finally Sammy nodded.

"Yeah, okay."

Lia put lids on the coffees and handed them to the older woman. "Here you go."

"Thanks," the older woman said. "The antique store closes at three, Izzy, but you can stay here and talk with your friend if you want."

"I have to work," Sammy said, not exactly unkindly, but definitely not inviting any *talk*.

"Okay. Well, see you tomorrow," Izzy said, unfazed. She waved to Sammy as the two left, and Sammy waved awkwardly back.

Lia watched the pair exit the bakery, then turn in the direction of the antique store. The girl grinned up at the woman, clearly enjoying their muffin and coffee and *time* together, and Lia felt an odd, softhearted pang.

"Well, that was terrible," Sammy said miserably once they were out of sight.

Lia looked at the teen dubiously. "Yeah, she seemed so *cruel*."

"You don't know what it's like," Sammy said, miserably and cryptically all at the same time.

"What *what's* like?"

"Having to hide everything so no one finds out who you really are."

Yeah, Lia actually knew *exactly* what that was like. Maybe not at fifteen, in fairness. But not far off that. Of course, Sammy wasn't in witness protection, so she meant it in the teenage-angst way.

"Who you are isn't half bad, Sammy," Lia said firmly.

Sammy clearly did not see this as a *compliment* or even something that needed to be said. "Yeah, but when people start asking questions about *parents*, things get real bad, real quick. Deadbeat dad I never knew. Teen drug-addicted mom. Everyone's out then."

Okay, maybe *not* average teenage angst. Still. "I'm sure there are other kids with crappy parents," Lia said.

But Sammy clearly didn't agree, because she went and got the supplies to clean the tables and actually got to work without Lia having to harp on her anymore.

So, Lia did her end-of-day tasks. Maybe it wasn't her place, but she'd make sure Gard knew about the invitation so he could encourage Sammy to take it. The girl might be worried about how the truth of her parents would affect relationships, but she needed friends her own age.

Lia knew how important that was. To find people who… felt safe. And teenage girls were a whole thing, no doubt there'd be drama, but it should be…fifteen-year-old drama. Not adult drama.

Lia had learned that one the hard way.

Like clockwork, Gard entered the bakery right at three, dressed in his uniform. No matter how many days she saw it, Lia's heart did an obnoxious flutter. Worse as the days went on, because now she knew he'd stay and chat.

Flirt.

She liked to think she'd remained strong, but the fact of the matter was, it wasn't hard to remain strong when the guy never made a move. Sure, he flashed her that knee-melting grin. Said something with a little innuendo that had her cheeks heating and her imagination running away with her.

But he didn't ask her out. He asked her what kind of music she listened to, what movies she liked. He asked pertinent questions about the bakery business. He told her funny stories about his day—never getting into the nitty-gritty, though she was beginning to recognize that *bad day* look in his eyes.

But he didn't ask her out. Which was *good.*

"We need to go by the store on our way home," Sammy told Gard. "I've got a recipe I want to make tonight."

"Sure." Gard leaned against the counter Lia stood behind. "I've certainly been well-fed lately."

Sammy walked out the door, nose to her phone, but Gard lingered. Not uncommon. If they needed to discuss something a little…touchy regarding Sammy, this was the time to do it.

So Lia jumped in, because even with a counter between them, with him leaning against it he felt…close. So Lia kept her gaze on Sammy outside the big storefront window, typing away on that phone. "So, um. This girl Sammy knew came by and invited Sammy to get help with some homework before school starts tomorrow. Sammy said she'd go, but I just wanted to… She should go. Make sure she goes. The girl seemed nice. Studious."

"Two of my favorite words for people who want to be friends with Sammy. Yeah, I can get her to school early if she can drag herself out of bed."

"Good." Lia lifted her gaze from Sammy to Gard's blue gaze. *Damn.* She had to focus. "She's a good kid." Which was an inane thing to say since she knew he agreed.

"Yeah, and she's got you wrapped around her finger."

Lia bristled. "Not any more than she has you."

"Wanna bet?"

She served him a disapproving look. Hopefully. "And just how would either of us prove this bet?"

"I don't know. I'll figure something out." He studied her then, in that way that had her pulse jangling like she'd never talked to an attractive man before when she certainly *had.*

"So, when am I going to be making this up to you?"

Something complicated twisted in Lia's chest. She didn't like him treating it like a…transaction. Like she was doing anything to be *owed*. "I'm not helping her for you," she said resolutely.

"I know. You're doing it for her, but that in turn is doing something for me. So…"

"So…what?"

"How about—"

The bell jangled violently on the door. Sammy stuck her head in. "Are you *coming*?"

Gard blew out a breath, something Lia couldn't quite read flickering in those blue eyes. But he smiled at her, and he didn't finish whatever he'd been about to say. "See you later, Lia."

"Yeah." She blew out a breath of her own, because she'd gotten the distinct feeling that maybe that *How about*…had been the start of some kind of invitation.

And *not* about Sammy.

Which led her to have to admit to herself that if he'd asked her out in that moment, direct blue eyes and ridiculous intent expression, she would have said yes.

And then she would have regretted it and probably backed out.

But first, she would have said yes.

Chapter Six

The three-week mark of Sammy working for Lia at the bakery came and went. No one mentioned it, and Sammy kept going. Sometimes she met her new friends after school there, and Lia let them stay after hours. Gard would pick her up, and Sammy would be flushed with pleasure, homework done, talking a mile a minute about anything and everything.

He could almost set aside the gaping absence of Dani. Sammy was happy. That was what mattered.

But any free moment at work, Gard checked in on Beckett's human trafficking case or poked at the old wounds he couldn't seem to let heal.

But if he ever got it in his head to *do* something, he thought of the way Sammy had cried all over him and been so upset he'd been looking for Dani. So he kept his investigation well under wraps, and nothing outside of work boundaries and hours.

This afternoon, Gard's zone was in Fairmont, and he still hadn't been assigned a new recruit yet, so he was on his own. He'd answered a few calls, but the radio was quiet now and he just…happened to pass the restaurant where Dani had been working the past two years.

They were a kind of diner, so he could certainly stop

by and pick up a cup of coffee to go. Nothing wrong with that. And if he *happened* to ask anyone who'd worked with Dani if they'd heard from her, it wasn't using company time for personal business, because it was just a quick coffee break. And it wasn't *looking* for Dani, because he was just getting coffee.

You're really splitting hairs.

He got out of the car anyway. The day was cool, the air in the diner warm and smelling of bacon and stale coffee. The murmur of conversation paused when he stepped inside, but when the customers realized he was just heading to the counter to order, it started up again.

The woman who took his order wasn't wearing a name tag, so he didn't know if she was one of the women Dani might have mentioned over the past two years, but…what the hell? He didn't have to *do* anything with the answers to his questions. *If* he even got them.

Gard smiled at the woman, trying to adopt a friendly manner. "Hey, I was looking for the day manager. I need to ask her a few questions if she's got a minute."

"That's me." The woman sized him up quickly. "Are you Dani's brother?"

Gard's smile faded. "Yeah, how'd you know?"

"She said her brother was a cop and *Fairhurst* isn't exactly a common last name," the woman said, gesturing at his nameplate. "Is this about Dani?"

Gard tried to keep his expression neutral. "Sort of. I was wondering when the last time you'd seen her was."

"The afternoon she quit. What was that? A month ago?"

"Wait." Gard's heartbeat sped up as he absorbed this brand-new information. "She quit her job here?"

"Yeah. I take it she didn't tell you."

"No." And it left him…concerned, worried. Another

check in the *abnormal* column he kept promising himself he wasn't going to fall for. Because she could have quit right before she disappeared because she'd already known she was falling back into old habits.

But it could also be…more. "Can you tell me what she told you about quitting?"

"She was apologetic, but she said she'd been offered a better job. She also told me she'd still cover some shifts if I needed her to, if it didn't interfere with the new job. So I called her a few times since we're always short-staffed. I left some messages, but I haven't heard from her."

Nothing about this was out of the ordinary. Sure, he was surprised Dani would quit because her job here had been the longest she'd ever been able to hold down—mostly because of the woman across from him. Dani had actually gotten along with her manager for once.

But why hadn't she told him she quit? That she got a new job? He hadn't even known she'd been looking for something different. Was this about the lack of money she'd been complaining about that Sammy had mentioned?

Maybe she'd been using for a while and he and Sammy hadn't seen the signs. Maybe Dani had hidden it even better than usual.

Which meant he should *stop* this. Instead, he asked more questions. "Do you know anything about this new job? Where it is or what it was?"

The manager shook her head. "Not really. All I know is that one of our customers offered it to her."

A customer. So, not a lie. Something real. But hell if it didn't sound fishy. And again, not unlike Dani to fall for something fishy. Because if it was on the up and up, she would have told him about it. So this wasn't *abnormal*. It was right on track with her behavior when she was using.

And still, he didn't let it go. "Do you think you could get me the name of that customer?"

"One of my waitresses might know." The woman's expression was serious. She leaned forward. "Is Dani okay?" she asked in a low voice.

Gard hesitated. He didn't want too many people to know she was missing. But… There was just too much potential the people who worked here might have a lead, especially if Dani talked to any of them about this new job. "I'm not sure. I haven't been able to get a hold of her. So I'm trying to track her down and make sure she's okay. Anything you can tell me would be a big help."

"I'll ask around. See if she told any of the girls she worked with about it. Do you want to wait, or…"

God, did he, but he had work to do, and Sammy would not approve of any of this. Better to treat it as a nonemergency. Since that's what it was. All it could be.

He pulled his business card out of his wallet. He scribbled his cell number on the back. "Call me with anything you find out. Please."

"Sure. Dani talked about you and that daughter of hers like you two hung the moon. I'll help however I can. She's a sweetheart."

Yeah, she could be. When she wasn't using.

But if she'd had a new job… Better pay? Enough to quit the restaurant? How would drugs factor in?

There were drugs in that house. Don't let this fool you.

He wouldn't. No. No getting his hopes up. Just…doing his due diligence. So that when Dani came crawling back, he could help her in whatever ways she needed.

No getting his nose broken this time. No upsetting Sammy. Just…preparing for what might come next.

That was all.

WHEN THE BELL on the door tinkled, Sammy jumped to attention.

Lia scowled at the girl. Oh *that* she heard, but not Albennie telling her three times to sift the flour before putting it in the batter.

Albennie had left for the day with that *knowing* look. *You're a softy, Lia Blair.*

Sammy turned to Lia, hands clasped—her phone in between her palms. "Can I work the register? *Please.*"

Suspicious at Sammy's sudden interest in doing *anything* not directly connected to that phone, Lia moved so she could see out into the storefront. Sammy's friends, Izzy and Sarabeth, came in, chattering excitedly.

Sammy slid past Lia, not waiting for Lia's answer. "You got it?" she demanded of the girls.

Sarabeth—by far the most extroverted and talkative of the three—did a full-blown jig. "I'm a licensed driver! Mom said I have to bring the car back by four, and I'm only allowed one friend at a time since you guys aren't licensed drivers, so we're just going to have to hang out here, but still! I drove over here all by myself."

Lia watched the girls talk excitedly about this development. It was a sweet, very normal teenage thing, and it made her heart ache. She was so glad Sammy got to have this moment. She only wished she could have more like it, uncomplicated by *life.*

But Sammy had told Lia, at least in vague terms, that these girls who'd become her friends had just as bad—if not worse—parental stories than she did, though they were both now in more stable situations than Sammy was. Though Lia didn't think Sammy understood just how lucky she was to have that uncle of hers.

"It sounds like you girls should celebrate," Lia said. All

three heads turned to her. "Cupcakes on the house. Sammy, get the cupcakes then go ahead and take a break with your friends."

"Really?"

"Really."

Sammy did a little jig of her own, talking animatedly about school-related things while she plated up cupcakes for her friends. Lia went back into the kitchen, retrieved her purse, and pulled out cash to cover the treats. She'd add it to the till later, but she put it in her pocket so she'd remember.

When the bell on the door rang again, she glanced at the clock. Three. No doubt it was Gard. Lia didn't rush out, though there was always that kind of knee-jerk reaction to *want* to.

She liked watching the way Sammy brightened. The way *Gard* brightened when he arrived. Like they were always a little relieved the other was exactly where they were supposed to be.

It somehow made her both terribly sad that they worried, and heartwarmingly happy that they had each other. Lia knew all too well what it was like to have no one at all.

So she could only resist for a moment or two before she left the kitchen. Besides, it didn't *have* to be Gard. It could be a customer.

But of course it was him. Standing there in his uniform. Looking at Sarabeth with a mix of amusement and trepidation—which was usually how Lia felt about the confident teenager.

"Sammy doesn't think you'll let her go to my birthday party," Sarabeth was saying to Gard.

"Well, she's probably right."

Sarabeth shook her head—not like she was upset with

his answer, more like she was disappointed in him. She held out a piece of paper.

"This is my mom's cell phone number. I'll tell her you're going to call her, and you can ask whatever questions you want. It's just going to be pizza and cake—coed at my house, then a few of the girls are going to sleep over."

Lia watched with interest as Gard looked down at the paper with a pained expression. He didn't want to say yes, but Lia had a feeling he was about to have the fight of his life on his hands—while Izzy and Sammy watched from their table, nothing but crumbs left from their cupcakes.

"Plus, my stepdad's brother's wife's cousin is Thomas Hart, and he works at Bent County too. He's a detective, so you probably know him." Sarabeth didn't show so much of a hesitation in reciting that complicated and convoluted connection to a detective.

"*And* my baseball coach's wife's sister is married to Copeland Beckett," Sarabeth continued. "He's a detective too."

"Yeah, I know the detectives, but that doesn't—"

"Oh, and Izzy's uncle is the sheriff of Sunrise." She gestured back at the table at Izzy. "*And* her aunt is Chloe Hudson. She works in the K9 unit at Bent County."

"Yeah, I know Sheriff and Deputy Hudson," Gard said firmly.

"Plus *plus* her other uncle is the fire invest—"

"You guys being randomly connected to a bunch of cops doesn't change the fact that…a sleepover with people I don't know at a place I don't know might not be in the cards for next weekend."

"Yeah, but you can ask all those trustworthy adults if *I'm* trustworthy." Sarabeth smiled winningly at him. "Izzy's dad is *super* overprotective, and he lets her spend the night sometimes. And my parents are always there, plus my aunt and uncle and…"

Gard looked over at Lia while Sarabeth chattered on about her living arrangements. Lia didn't like how she felt when he did that. Like she was somehow part of this, when she *wasn't*. It reminded her of that day when Sammy had cried about his nose, and he'd looked so helpless.

Sure, Lia had once *been* a teenage girl, but she'd never been a parent. Maybe Gard wasn't Sammy's *parent*, but he'd certainly been helping to take care of her for a long time.

"Okay," Gard finally said, cutting off Sarabeth. "I'll… call your mom tonight and we'll go from there."

"Great!" Sarabeth immediately turned back to the other girls. They leaned their heads together around the table in hushed tones, while Gard stared at them a bit like he'd been flattened by a steamroller.

The Sarabeth Thompson experience.

He shook his head, then turned toward her. Lia had to brace herself, because she was learning it was way too easy to get lost in conversation with Gard Fairhurst.

Before he could say anything to her, the girls were getting up from their table.

"I'll be outside," Sammy called, stepping out with her friends.

"I know they're good kids. But a party? A *sleepover*?" he grumbled.

Lia sighed wistfully, maybe laying it on a little thick, but while she understood Gard's concerns, she was 100 percent on Sammy's side for this one. "I would have killed to be in the kind of place at fifteen where I could have even been invited to a sleepover, let alone go."

He eyed her. "And what kind of place were you in that you couldn't?"

He didn't very often ask direct questions. Sometimes he hinted around, but nothing like this. She wasn't really supposed to *answer* direct questions about the *before*.

But maybe if he understood there *was* worse out there, he could understand that Sammy deserved to be as normal as he could give her. Which, no, that wasn't fair. She knew he wanted her to feel normal. He just worried, which was sweet.

But he didn't always realize when it got in the way of Sammy's happiness. So she held his gaze, and said as matter-of-factly as she could, "I ran away from home when I was fifteen."

His gaze stayed steady. There was no surprise in his expression, though surely it surprised him a little. "Fifteen, huh?"

She held that steady gaze. "I never went back."

"That bad?"

Lia considered, not sure why she was being so damn honest. He just seemed to bring it out in her. "Looking back? Probably not. But it felt that bad at the time."

Gard let out a long breath.

"How about you? Was it all that bad?" She meant for his sister, but maybe for him too. Because Lia was an only child, so she didn't understand how the same situation could create a police officer like Gard—all good and noble, and somcone who would abandon their daughter.

Maybe that should just be chalked up to drugs. Addiction. She'd been around enough of both to know addiction didn't discriminate.

Gard glanced out the window at Sammy and her friends standing on the sidewalk. "Looking back? I wonder if I'd realized how bad it was earlier, if things would be different for them."

"Like what?"

He turned to her then, slight smile on his face, but those blue eyes intense. "For that information, Lia Blair, I think you're going to have to come out to dinner with us."

Before she could fully analyze that sentence, and the way her heart jittered in her chest in ways she didn't remember *ever* feeling, he continued.

"Every Saturday night, if Sammy did all her homework for the week and didn't commit any crimes, we go for pizza. The *didn't commit any crimes* stipulation is new this year. I thought it went without saying, but it apparently had to be said. You should come with us tonight."

Oh, she absolutely should not. Especially since she was sharing secrets she shouldn't.

Not that it was like…a date. Sammy was going to be there. It was just a friendly invite. They were all…friends.

"Six o'clock at HJs in Fairmont. Meet us if you can." He took a step back from the counter, then another, holding her gaze as he backed away. *Clearly* enjoying himself and what had to be the shell-shocked expression on her face.

Then he turned and walked out the bakery door.

And Lia knew she would spend the next hour going back and forth, knowing she shouldn't go, but wanting to.

Chapter Seven

"You invited Lia?" Sammy repeated, clearly surprised as they drove into Fairmont. They'd gone home and Gard had showered the day off of him. Sammy had, wisely, not brought up the party or calling Sarabeth's mom.

She *would*, but the girl knew how to time things when she wanted to. Like the current question.

"Yeah, I did. That okay?"

"Uh, *yeah*, but…" She trailed off. He could *feel* her narrow-eyed stare. "You're just trying to put off calling Sarabeth's mom."

Maybe. But it was a hell of an excuse. He was also using it as an excuse to distract himself from the fact he was waiting for a call or text from Dani's manager at the restaurant with the name of whatever customer had offered her a job.

"Look, I'll call her," Gard said reluctantly. "I promise. I'm glad you have friends you want to hang out with." He wasn't *really*, but he knew he *should* be. "Were you friends with them last year?"

Sammy sat back in the seat, maybe looking *almost* mollified. "I kind of avoided making friends last year. It's not like Mom could have driven me places or whatever with her work schedule, and she got all weird if I had *guy* friends."

"Count me among the getting weird if you have guy friends. Why is this party coed, by the way?"

Sammy rolled her eyes. "We're *sixteen*, Gard. Not babies."

He didn't point out that while Sarabeth had turned sixteen, Izzy and Sammy had yet to join her there. Because Sammy was still talking, and maybe fifteen wasn't *babies* either, but still…

"Besides, Sarabeth plays softball *and* baseball. She's really good. The boys are just her baseball teammates—at least the ones who aren't jerks. And her parents won't let boys sleep over, even though Sarabeth gave them this big presentation on how it's totally sexist gender essentialism to ban an entire gender."

Well, at least Sarabeth's parents sounded like reasonable people. He definitely wasn't going to ask what gender essentialism was though. He'd look it up it later. Or maybe he'd live in ignorant bliss.

"Besides, if you let me go, it's the perfect excuse. You can finally ask Lia out. Just you and her."

Gard choked on his own saliva since he hadn't seen *that* segue coming. "Excuse me?"

Sammy waved a dramatic arm. "Oh, please, like it's not obvious you want to."

"Sammy." He had no idea what to say to that. What he *should* say. They did not…discuss his personal life.

"*And* she wants you to," Lia added.

Gard desperately *wanted* to demand how she knew that. But he was *not* a teenager, and neither was Lia. This wasn't high school. He was Sammy's guardian, which meant this wasn't about him and Lia. It was about…her.

"Why are you matchmaking?" he asked, trying to sound reasonable and unaffected.

"Why not?"

"I can handle my own dates, Sammy. It may shock you to know, but women tend to find me attractive."

She groaned and made a vomit gesture. "Whatever. The point is, if *I'm* what's holding you back on that score, I shouldn't be."

"You're never holding me back, Sam."

"You don't have to lie."

He pulled into the parking lot of the restaurant, shoved the truck into Park, then twisted in his seat so he could look directly at her, without the distraction of driving.

"Sammy, I have a lot of complicated and conflicting feelings about everything that has gone on in your mother's life, and in yours, but you have never—not *once*—been something that held me back. I have exactly the life I want, and that includes taking care of you."

She didn't meet his gaze. But after a few beats of silence, she spoke very softly. "Mom would always… She said she couldn't date while I was underfoot."

Gard wished Dani would have phrased that better for Sammy, but… "Your mom had good reasons for that rule."

Sammy slid a glance at him then. "Because of my dad?"

Gard sighed, not sure how everything had devolved into *this*. But he wasn't going to lie to her. "Look, your dad was a… He was young and he was dumb, and boy was he damn selfish, but he wasn't mean. A couple of the guys she was involved with after? Mean." And dangerous. Not just for Dani, but for Sammy too.

If there was one thing his sister had gotten right, it was swearing off men for the past ten years.

"Lia's not mean."

Gard wanted to groan. "Sammy."

"You like her. You think she's hot."

"We're not talking about this." Though even awkward and kind of weird, better than talking about Dani's bad dating choices.

"Don't not have a life because of me," she told him earnestly.

"Don't worry, I didn't have a life before you came into the picture either." Probably not the best argument either.

"More of one."

Maybe, but not by much.

"Look, if I end up letting you go to that party, it'll be *for* you. So *you* can have fun with your friends in a safe environment. It won't be about what I want to do while you're somewhere else."

"But that's what I'm saying. You should do stuff for yourself too. Don't forget, I was there when Matilda told Mom *and* you that your entire lives can't revolve around me."

Gard scowled at the invocation of the family therapist. Who likely would also side on letting Sammy go to this party. Doing *normal* things, rather than feeling like she was being punished

Damn it.

He remembered what Lia had said about wishing she'd been in a place to be able to go to sleepovers.

Fifteen. He'd been obsessed with sports and trying to talk Madison Sealy behind the bleachers. And Lia had run away and never gone back.

Before he could figure out anything else to say to Sammy to get it through her head she was no burden, another car turned into the parking lot. It was an old junker of a car, but he quickly recognized Lia in the driver's seat.

He grinned in spite of himself.

She'd come.

Lia didn't know why she was here, but the fact Gard and Sammy were smiling at her as she approached made it feel like the right choice.

She had friends. But they were all Hope Town friends. All with their own secret pasts. They had busy lives, trying to handle small business in a small town. It made it easier to understand each other, trust each other and the town they were building, but it didn't quite make for…deep connections. Just because you knew each other had secrets didn't mean you could share them.

Not that she could have any deep relationship with Gard or Sammy, because they couldn't know the truth about her.

But they didn't know…*any of it*—not that she wasn't Lia Blair, not that she *had* secrets, so this didn't feel like… anything else in her life. It felt like a fresh start. It felt like making Lia Blair…real, instead of a role she was inhabiting.

Of course, now Gard knew she was a teenage runaway, but that wasn't particularly identifying. So, it was okay. It was all okay.

So why are you so damn nervous? And more importantly, why are you here?

Sammy greeted her with a hug, and Lia supposed that answered her question. Sure, there was this whole weird… flirty thing with Gard, but at the end of the day, she'd fallen for Sammy hard. It wasn't just that she wanted to help a girl who reminded her of herself, it was that Sammy was… great. And Lia wanted to be a part of that.

They went into the pizza place and got a booth. If Lia wasn't *totally* off base, Sammy was trying to finagle Lia to have to sit next to Gard, but Lia purposefully sat at the edge of one side of the booth so that no one could sit with her. Sammy pouted.

Lia's nerves intensified, because if that girl was trying to make something happen between her and Gard…

But Sammy picked up the menu and fixed Lia with a direct glare. "What kind of pizza toppings do you like?"

"I'm pretty easy. Nothing fishy and no mushrooms. Otherwise, I'm open to anything."

"Oh, don't say that," Gard muttered.

"Okay," Sammy said, shooting Gard a triumphant grin. "The arugula and caramelized onion with balsamic it is."

"Wait. Balsamic?" Lia pulled a face. "On pizza?"

"Thank you," Gard said emphatically. "See? No one wants that."

Sammy pouted again. "It's *sophisticated*. Uncle Gard has no *vision*," Sammy said. "Be on my side."

Lia looked from Gard to Sammy. "Sorry. I can't. I think I'd rather suffer through a mushroom."

Sammy rolled her eyes dramatically. "Someday, when I'm as far out of Wyoming as you can get, I will find people who appreciate *real* food."

Lia couldn't help but smile at the dramatics, but Gard wasn't smiling. Lia realized he was probably thinking about Sammy talking about leaving Wyoming, and how a few years would pass by in the blink of an eye.

Ouch.

They ordered. One meat lovers for Gard and Lia to share, and Sammy got a personal-pan pizza for her, as Gard called it, abomination. Gard made Sammy talk about what she'd learned in school, and though Sammy pretended to be irritated, Lia could see how much she enjoyed Gard's questions. His attention. *Him.*

"Sarabeth is trying to talk me into joining debate, but she's almost never there because of her sports schedule. I don't really know anyone else on the team, and Mr. Nielson is kind of a jerk."

"But you'd be good at it," Lia said encouragingly. "I'm pretty sure if you and Sarabeth teamed up, you'd be unstoppable."

Gard chuckled. "Debating *is* in the Fairhurst blood."

Sammy wrinkled her nose. "Well, I don't want to be like *them.*"

Gard ran a hand over her hair. "Never, kid."

Leaving Lia to wonder just what was wrong with the Fairhurst family.

"You know, before she dropped out, even your mom went to a state competition for debate," Gard told her.

"And you went to nationals. Yeah, yeah, yeah." Sammy turned her gaze onto Lia. "He's freaky smart. He was going to go to law school."

Gard shifted, clearly uncomfortable with that tidbit. Which Lia had to admit, made her want to hear more about it.

"Is that so?" Lia replied. She could see it though. It was easy to picture him all slicked back in a power suit. Talking people into or out of things, depending on what kind of lawyer. He had that…presence about him.

"Another family tradition," Gard said, a hint of bitterness in his tone. "Luckily, I decided to enforce the law instead of warp it even more." His phone trilled before he could say anything else. "Sorry. It's work. I have to take this. I'll be right back." He slid out of the booth and stepped outside the restaurant, but they could still see him through the window.

Lia noted Sammy was frowning as he talked seriously to whoever had given him a call. Then she turned her gaze on Lia—direct and blue, just like her uncle's.

"If he asks you out, you'd say yes, right?"

Lia felt a bit like she'd been slapped. There was certainly an odd ringing in her ears. "What?"

"Like on a date. You would, right?"

Her cheeks were burning, which was *ridiculous*, considering she was being questioned by a teenager. "What are you talking about?"

"Well, you like him, don't you?"

"Sammy, I… Sure. He's a nice guy, but that doesn't mean…" She looked helplessly at Gard, but he was tied up in his phone conversation. And there was this whole… dinner, and the other day when she'd thought… She leaned forward, lowered her voice. "Did he *say* he was going to ask me out?"

"Not in so many words," Sammy said. "He has this annoying tendency of, you know, not living his life when I'm around. And you're not…unlike that, though it's not about me, I know."

"I'm living my life," Lia said, not sure why she felt *offended* by a fifteen-year-old's point of view.

Sammy studied her critically. "You just seem really… alone."

Lia bristled, both in surprise and hurt. "I'm not alone."

"Albennie and Franny are the only two people I ever see you talk to."

Which wasn't…far off the truth. Sure, there were the business meetings with Zach and the other Hope Town business owners, and the book club at the bookstore when she managed to read the book, but…yeah mostly just Albennie and Franny and mostly just at the bakery.

But *Sammy* didn't need to know that. "Sammy, that's very…sweet that you're concerned, but you only see a fraction of my life. I have a lot of responsibilities outside the bakery, and other friends. A whole, full life." Sort of.

Sammy frowned a little, clearly considering for the first time Lia might have a life outside of when Sammy saw her. But then she looked over at Gard, who was still outside talking on his phone.

"What's wrong with him?" Sammy asked.

"Nothing is *wrong* with him." Like, literally nothing. And wasn't that a problem? "I'm just not…big on dating."

"Why not?"

Because I have a secret past and you can't really build a relationship on lies.

"Sammy, this is sweet, but…"

"Just, if he asks, give him a chance. He needs someone. Maybe you're not alone and lonely, but *he* is."

"Did he say that?"

Sammy snorted. "He's a *guy*, Lia. He doesn't realize it yet."

Lia studied the teen, knowing she couldn't argue with *that*. Still… This was a lot. She reached across the table, put her hand over Sammy's.

"Sammy, you mean a lot to me. I wouldn't want to complicate…anything."

"It's not complicated. I like you both. You like each other. If he's a jerk, I'll key his truck for you. If you're a jerk, I'll switch all the sugar in the bakery out for salt." Sammy shrugged as if anything was that simple. "Look, he's coming. Don't tell him I said anything. Just say yes if he asks, okay?"

But Lia couldn't agree or disagree because Gard was back, sliding into his seat.

"You don't have to go in to work, do you?" Sammy asked.

Gard smiled, but Lia saw some tension behind it. She figured Sammy did too. "No. Not heading into work."

Chapter Eight

They walked out of the restaurant stuffed, and Gard had been able to mostly forget the phone call from Dani's former manager.

He had a name for the customer who'd gotten Dani the alleged new job. What he'd *wanted* to do was ditch dinner. Honestly, if Lia hadn't come, he would have hurried Sammy along and done just that. But the presence of another person had made him think twice.

And reminded him that Sammy was his priority. Not *maybe* tracking down whatever hole Dani had jumped into of her own accord.

So, he owed Lia his thanks, even if she didn't know it. And it had been…nice. To not just be the two of them. Sammy kind of performed for him, but with another adult there she had relaxed more into herself.

Or maybe just with *Lia* there, she relaxed more into herself.

Outside, the air was cool. Fall would turn into winter in the blink of an eye, that was for sure.

"You know what?" Sammy said. "I need to go to the bathroom. You guys wait here."

Gard watched her go back into the restaurant. He didn't buy that for a minute. But he couldn't exactly call her on it.

He looked back at Lia, who was also frowning at Sammy's retreating form, like she *also* knew what the girl was up to.

But then her gaze met his. Considering. "So, a lawyer, huh?"

He didn't wince, *exactly.* "That was the path." Sometimes, he could see it so clearly—walking in his father's footsteps, caring more about how he appeared and what his bank account said than who he was as a man.

Scared the hell out of him, and since he didn't want to think about that, he turned it around on her. "And what were your plans?"

Lia looked out at the setting sun. She blew out a breath. "I've pretty much had two plans in my life," she said, clearly contemplating. "Escape. Survive." She didn't meet his gaze, but she was clearly being honest.

"Sounds rough."

She shook her head, as if shaking the seriousness away. She smiled. "I guess I'm doing more than survive these days. Just…took me a while to realize it."

"I get that. Probably not for the same reasons, but when Sammy was little everything felt like just…making it to the next day in one piece." And even when he hadn't been in charge of Sammy, he'd worried. So there hadn't been a reprieve, really.

"She's very lucky to have you," Lia said very seriously, making it crystal clear that she'd been a runaway teen because she hadn't had *anyone.*

"Well, I failed her mom pretty big-time, so we'll call it even if I can get her to graduation in one piece. And not pregnant. God, I've just tempted the universe by saying that out loud."

Some of Lia's seriousness lifted into humor. "I think

you'll be okay. She's hurting, but she loves you. She wants to make you proud."

Gard wasn't sure that was fully true, but it wasn't fully *untrue*. More than that, he didn't want Sammy to worry about making *him* proud. "As long as she's proud of herself, that's what matters."

Lia didn't say anything to that, but her eyes got kind of shiny, like a person's did when they were about to cry. And while he dealt with tears at work, with Dani, with Sammy, he wasn't sure he was in a place to deal with *Lia's* tears.

"Sounds like you two have gotten to be friends," Gard said, changing the subject. Wanting to see her smile.

"I like to think so."

"And it sounds like you think I make Sammy happy."

Lia's eyes narrowed, like she knew where he was going with this. "You do."

"So, if I make one of your friends happy… Sounds like you might be forced to like me in spite of my uniform."

"Hmm," she said.

But she was messing with him. He could see it in her eyes. And since she *was*… "Being a guardian is ninety-nine percent worry, so if I let Sammy go to this sleepover, I'm going to need something to…distract me from thinking about her being at a *party*. With *boys*."

Lia studied him. "Maybe you can go to work," she offered, and he knew she was purposefully ignoring his hint. Messing with him a little bit. Because if she was *uncomfortable* with the hint, she wouldn't be looking at him with that half smile on her face.

"Maybe. Maybe you could have dinner with me. Get me through the coed portion of the night."

She didn't answer right away. He hadn't really expected her to. Lia was too complicated for a simple yes or no.

Something that should probably send him running. Didn't he have enough complications?

But he could hardly help it if he was drawn to them.

"You know, I once made a promise to myself to never date cops," she said.

"Sounds like the kind of promise made to be broken."

This time she did laugh. He liked her laugh. It always started soft, and then she'd lean into it, as if being reminded she *did* know how.

He had the very strong desire to remind her. Over and over.

"Maybe." She studied him critically. "Tell me one thing. What was that work phone call about?"

He glanced back at the restaurant. Sighed. "If I tell you, you have to be cool with not telling Sammy."

She wrinkled her nose. "It was about her mom?"

"Sort of. Nothing bad. Nothing, really. Just…"

"You trying to find her even though Sammy doesn't want you to?"

Yeah, that was pretty much it. "I love Sammy, and I'd do anything for her, but Dani is my sister. I'm trying really hard to put Sammy first, because it's what she deserves, *and* what Dani would want, but… I wasn't there when Dani was first starting to struggle. I was off at college enjoying all the perks of being Gardner Elliot Fairhurst *the Fourth*. I can't fail her like that again. I can't just let it go she's out there ruining her own life again. I have to try to…do something."

"You don't have to justify it to me, Gard," Lia said softly.

But at the same time Lia was saying that, loosening something tied tight inside of him, he heard Sammy's voice. He turned toward her hurrying out of the restaurant.

She looked pale. Gard's heart dropped. He moved toward her immediately.

"What's wrong? Are you okay? Did you get sick?"

She just held out her phone. He looked at the screen in confusion. It was open to her text messages. And at the top of the list was one from *Mom*.

Gard's heart pounded in his ears. Dani had finally reached out. She was *okay*. He wanted to feel relief. And he did, but there was a twinge of anger with it. Because all Dani had texted was: sorry.

"It's just my mom. *Finally* texting me," Sammy explained to Lia. Her voice was a little overloud as she rolled her eyes, but they were shiny and the way she shrugged was jerky. A lot more than her usual teenage disgust. This was hurt. "Whatever." She grabbed her phone from Gard then marched away, toward Gard's car.

Gard raked a hand through his hair, blew a shaky breath out. Dani was okay. Okay enough to text. To communicate. God, his knees felt weak.

Lia reached out, gave his arm a squeeze. "I'll see you tomorrow when you drop her off."

Gard managed to nod. Wished he could hold on to this moment, but he couldn't. He had to hold on to Sammy while she worked her way through this. "Yeah. Tomorrow."

LIA HADN'T SLEPT WELL. She'd tossed and turned, worrying about Sammy and Gard. She'd written—and then deleted, unsent—multiple text messages to both of them.

She'd also spent an obscene amount of time talking herself out of googling *Gardner Elliot Fairhurst the Fourth*. Law school. Plans. She'd maybe assumed his life had been a little hardscrabble, but with a name like that and a past like that?

No, she knew the type a little too well. It should be yet another turnoff in a long list of them.

Somehow it wasn't.

Lia got up when her alarm went off, groaned even though she'd been awake anyway. The mornings were getting close to frigid, so she drove over to the bakery rather than walking. The lights were on, Albennie already working in the kitchen, headphones on.

No breaking the no-talking rule this morning, which was good because Lia was grumpier than usual, wrung out with anxiety. She was worried about Sammy *and* Gard, and until she saw them this band of anxiety was going to be wrapped around her.

Instead, it got tighter and tighter, because Gard was *always* on time, but the clock kept inching past six. Later and later and later.

Maybe she should call. Or maybe they'd overslept. Maybe they needed the time. Maybe—

"Uh-oh," Albennie said softly. Lia looked to where she was gesturing.

Outside the storefront window, illuminated only by the streetlight and the light above the bakery exterior door, Gard and Sammy stood. Clearly arguing.

Lia's heart ached.

"You don't look surprised," Albennie said. "When *I've* never seen them fight."

"They had a rough night," Lia managed to say. "Stuff with Sammy's mom."

"You're awfully involved."

Lia tried not to feel defensive. Failed. "I'm just being a...friend."

"To which one?"

Lia couldn't quite take her gaze off them. Sammy was gesturing wildly. Fury was written all over her face. Gard was still, calm, maybe stoic even, but Lia could see the muscle tick in his jaw. "Both." No use denying it. Besides, she could be friends with both. She could…worry about them both.

"Well, I'll be in the kitchen. You can deal with…that."

Sammy threw her hands up in the air one more time and then stormed inside. She said *nothing* to Lia standing there behind the counter, but when Gard tried to say something to her, she didn't let him even get half a word out.

"I *hate* you," she yelled. Sammy slammed into the back room. Gard winced. Then looked apologetically at Lia.

"I'm sorry. Maybe I should have let her stay home…" He trailed off, raking a hand through his hair. "I just don't want her alone right now. I know that's not your responsibility, but—"

"It's not my responsibility because it's my pleasure," Lia said firmly.

Gard snorted. "I can guarantee you it won't be a pleasure today."

No, probably not. Lia skirted the counter, feeling like she needed to…help somehow. "She doesn't hate you."

"No. I know. Family therapy for the win," he said, heavy with sarcasm. But he looked absolutely miserable. "We probably need some time apart anyway but please call me if she gets to be too much. I'll get someone to cover my shift. I'll…"

She put her hands on his arms, gave him a reassuring squeeze. "I've got this, Gard." She needed to impress that upon him. *She* could do this. For Sammy. For him.

He smiled. Or tried. "Thanks."

He didn't pull his arms away from her hands and he just looked so damn miserable—and exhausted—she didn't know what else to do except step closer, move those hands up his arms and around, and…just offer a supportive, *platonic* hug.

He seemed so alone right in this moment, and God knew she understood being alone, standing alone, handling it all *alone*.

His uniform was stiff. She could feel the hard press of his vest underneath the shirt. He smelled like laundry detergent. He felt tall and strong and so *sturdy*, but she knew he wasn't feeling all that sturdy right now.

"It's going to be okay," she said reassuringly, taking an awkward step back. Why had she given him a *hug*?

"Can I get that in writing?" he asked, a tiny bit of humor in his eyes that were otherwise very direct and very blue.

Her stomach jittered. Not that usual, easy flirty attraction. No, this was far more complicated a feeling. She *knew* this was all dangerous. She could feel it in every reaction inside of her, but she couldn't seem to stop herself.

"I need you to call me if things get to be too much though, okay?" he said, oh so seriously. "Promise me."

"All right. I promise." But she also promised herself there wouldn't be any *too much*. No matter how bad it got.

He nodded. "Good. I'll be back at three." He shot one helpless look in the direction of the kitchen then shook his head. "Good luck in there."

"Thanks."

Gard strode out. And Lia gave herself a minute, because her heart felt…weird and bruised in what was not a totally *bad* way. She just didn't understand what way it was.

When Lia forced herself to go into the kitchen, Albennie had her headphones on and was kneading dough. Sammy was staring at the open dishwasher. Her first job of the day was to empty it, but she wasn't doing that. She was just standing. Staring. A step up from looking at her phone, but only a step up.

"Do you want me to help you with that?"

Sammy fixed her with the most scathing glare. "I think I can handle unloading dishes, *thanks*."

The morning went a lot like that. Sammy dawdling—not in her normal ways though. There was no texting, no internet videos. There was a lot of standing around staring off into space. But if Lia suggested a job, or asked if she needed help, Sammy snapped her head off with cutting teenage sarcasm.

The bakery was packed today, like everyone had decided to enjoy one last outdoor day before winter swept in. Sammy refused to work the register, even though that was usually one of her favorite things to do.

"Oh, I didn't know we got to just *decide* to not do part of our jobs," Albennie said under her breath. Lia pretended not to hear it.

Hoping to maintain peace, Lia set Sammy up with a recipe to try while Lia went and manned the register. Almost an hour passed before she had a breath to pop in and check up on what was going on in the kitchen.

Albennie had her headphones on, shaping rolls. Sammy was standing next to the mixer, which was moving at high speed. But…she was crying.

Lia rushed over. "What's wrong?"

"I ruined it," Sammy said, shaking her head. "I accidentally did tablespoons. I'm such an idiot."

Lia turned off the mixer, gave Sammy's shoulder a squeeze. "No big deal. It happens."

"It *is* a big deal. I ruined it! It's all…ruined." She was sobbing now, and Lia didn't know what else to do but wrap her arms around Sammy and hold on. Albennie shot her a questioning look over Sammy's head, headphones around her neck now, but Lia didn't know what to do or how to explain.

"I've got the front if you want to…" Albennie gestured outside with her chin.

Lia nodded and started guiding Sammy out the back door. The wind was whipping around, cold and biting. So she led Sammy over to her car and gently nudged the girl into the passenger seat.

When she got into the driver's side, Sammy was leaning back in her seat. Her face was red and blotchy and wet, but it seemed like she'd actively stopped sobbing.

"Your car smells," she said in a squeaky voice.

"Sammy, sweetheart, I know you're having a hell of a time, and you're upset about your mom. You get to be that. And if you want to take it out on me? That's fine. I'm not going anywhere."

Sammy closed her eyes, looking exhausted and wrung out. "Whatever."

They sat in silence for a while. Lia handed Sammy a tissue and eventually she blew her nose, clearly starting to calm down. When she opened her eyes, she stared outside. "Why can't I be enough?" she asked, a few more tears trailing down her cheeks.

Lia didn't have any answers, because that had been a question she'd spent most of her life haunted by. *Why can't I be enough?* To make someone stay. Or care. Or anything.

Lia *wanted* to tell Sammy that she *was* enough. That she wasn't defined by the adults in her life or their decisions. She wanted to say a lot of things, but she knew from experience in a dark moment all those things just felt like platitudes.

She wanted to give Sammy something more than that. Something real and honest.

"You know, my parents…they died before I remember. And they'd lost custody of me even before that."

Sammy blinked over at her. There was some suspicion in that gaze, so Lia figured she had to lay it out. Really out. Maybe she wasn't supposed to, but none of these details were going to…fully give her past away.

"They were addicts. I'm not sure if they ever had custody of me, but if they did, it was brief. I was told I was with a grandparent when I was a baby, but then when I was two or three, I had to go live with my dad's brother and his wife. They always made sure I knew what happened to my parents—no sugarcoating there." Though Lia decided to sugarcoat a little by not mentioning to Sammy her parents had died of overdoses. "My aunt and uncle called them junkies. I always hated that."

Lia didn't expect Sammy to say anything to that, but she still paused, because she wasn't sure what she was trying to explain. Just that she understood. Just that…it wasn't as bad as the moment felt.

She knew. She *knew*.

"They were dead by the time I was old enough to understand, so there was no hope of them coming back. I don't know how it feels to deal with recovery and relapses. I won't pretend to. But I *do* understand that feeling of not being enough for anybody, because in that regard I never was."

"Was your uncle nice?" Sammy asked quietly.

"No. He was horrible. So was my aunt. So were my cousins. Not a one of them ever treated me like anything other than a burden on her way to being a *junkie,* just like her parents." She left out the part where she'd run away from it all at fifteen. Sammy probably didn't need any ideas in her head about running away.

"So you're saying I should be grateful I have Gard," Sammy said darkly.

"No," Lia replied. She *wanted* to say that, but she understood in dark moments people suggesting *gratefulness* never went over well. Besides, gratefulness often meant having the experience to realize you should be—and that was tough for any fifteen-year-old. "No, you don't have to be grateful, Sammy. You got dealt a terrible hand. You get to feel that. Having a decent adult in your life doesn't mean you can't be pissed off about the ones you don't have or the ways they've failed you. Because it's their failure. Not yours."

Sammy wiped at her cheeks with the back of her hands. "I keep trying to…accept it. That's what Matilda says. The goal is not change. It's *acceptance*."

Lia didn't know who Matilda was, but she nodded along, letting Sammy talk.

"Mom's always going to do this. She's always going to disappoint me. I'll never be enough to make her change, but things had been so good for so long, I forgot how to protect myself."

Lia reached out, wiped some of Sammy's tears off her cheeks herself. "There's protecting yourself and there's shutting down. Don't shut down. This sucks, and it hurts, but don't forget there are things that don't."

"Izzy and I…talk about it sometimes. Izzy's mom is the same, except… Izzy never really loved her mom because she was awful. And Sarabeth's dad was actually terrible too. I know that's worse, but…they get to hate the bad adult in their life. I just love mine. And I want her to come home, but she won't. Not for me. And I know, I know, it's not about *me*. It's about her. And drugs, but… I want her to come home. I want to be enough for her to make that choice, even if that's not…what it's about."

Lia was quiet for a few moments, because Sammy was certainly more mature than Lia had been at fifteen. Of course, Lia had been…in a much worse situation without *any* responsible adults. But maybe that meant Sammy was ready to hear some things Lia had been forced to learn on her own, in her early twenties instead of her teens.

"That feeling you have of not being enough? I don't know that it ever goes totally away, at least for me. But the more I have pursued the things I love and surrounded myself with people I love who love me back, the less it hurts, the less it matters. It's still there, it's still a truth in my darkest moments. But it's not the only thing."

Sammy looked over at Lia then. Lia didn't know if she'd really absorbed the words, but she *seemed* to consider them. So Lia went for broke.

"This is *your* life, not hers. You can't control her. Or anyone. But you can control you. So build a life that makes *you* happy. And when you're sad, there will be people there to hold your hand."

"If I don't treat them like crap," Sammy said, somewhat sarcastically.

Lia wanted to give her a smile, but… "I think you know your uncle will be holding your hand no matter how badly you treat him. But treating him like crap won't make you feel any better, so you might as well try not to."

Sammy blew out a long breath. "I just don't want it to hurt so much."

Lia took Sammy's hand in hers. Squeezed. "I know." There was nothing else to say to that. Didn't everybody wish that sometimes? But hurt was the human condition, because it was the other side of love.

Sammy reached across the center console and wrapped her arms around Lia and squeezed. So Lia squeezed back.

"I'm so glad I have you," Sammy said into her shoulder.

Lia had a hard time speaking through the lump in her throat. She hadn't expected…any of this when she'd offered Sammy a job all those weeks ago. She'd thought she was doing some Good Samaritan thing.

Instead, Sammy was…turning into this bright spot in Lia's own life, her own heart. "I'm glad I have you too."

"I'm sorry about today. I just…" Sammy pulled back, tears welling in her eyes again.

"I get it," Lia said firmly. "Sometimes when it hurts too much, a bad attitude is the only thing we've got. But you didn't ruin anything. Mistakes happen. We'll start over. No harm. No foul."

Sammy looked at the bakery's back entrance through the car window. Lia could see she was dreading going back inside.

Maybe she should force her to face it, but right now she just…wanted to give Sammy anything she wanted.

"You want to go for a drive?"

"Where?"

"I don't know. Just…drive."

"What about the bakery?"

"Albennie can handle it."

"Okay. Yeah." Her smile was tremulous, but it was a smile. So Lia texted Albennie, and she and Sammy drove around Bent County, listening to music and just…breathing. They didn't talk. Didn't have to.

It was good enough just to be.

Chapter Nine

Gard focused on work. His zone, not trafficking rings or Dani's shitty text message to Sammy or even the name the restaurant manager had given him.

Because he'd made a deal with himself when Sammy had cried all over him about his broken nose. Dani had contacted Sammy, no matter how cryptically, and that meant he couldn't keep poking into her disappearance.

She'd made her choices. She was alive. She'd come back when she was ready, and he'd deal with the aftermath. The end.

He really knew that should be the end. But the name the restaurant manager had given him was now stuck in his head.

What did it hurt to look into the guy? Just make sure he wasn't a criminal. That whatever job offer Dani had taken wasn't actively *hurting* her. It was only his due diligence—not breaking his promise to himself, because he wasn't *looking* for Dani.

He was just…checking on things. *Splitting hairs.*

But when had that ever stopped him?

Still, he waited until the end of his shift, when he was idling in his car at the station waiting to radio off and head out to Hope Town to pick up Sammy. He typed the guy's name into his system. No priors, which Gard could admit was a shock. Really, not much info on the guy at all.

Except a certain address—listed as *former*—that happened to be out on Dry Road.

Gard swore. Why was it all connecting? Of course, not in any way that offered a concrete answer. Not in any way that allowed him to rush in and save the day or give up in defeat. Just enough to keep him low-level worried and second-guessing himself.

The Dani Fairhurst Experience.

He looked up at the sheriff's department building, considering his options. Because this didn't...*mean* anything. This *job* she'd told her boss about could just be about drugs. With Dani, this kind of behavior was *always* about drugs. And years and years of dealing with it meant he knew—he *knew*—he could not do anything for her until she chose to do something for herself.

Asking around like it was ever going to be something else would likely lead to nothing but professional embarrassment. And certainly not helping Dani in any way.

He'd learned the hard way barreling in when she was using always made things worse for everyone involved. Early on, making demands, dragging her out of bad situations, it had only ever made Dani dig her heels in— meaning she stayed low and used longer.

She had to come to the decision to stop. *She* had to hit her rock bottom. Or Sammy got hurt worse. Every single time.

And still he got out of his car, walked into the building, and went in search of Detective Beckett.

He found the man in his office, clearly getting ready to leave for the day. Neither Hart nor Laurel were in the office with him, so Gard lucked out there. Just one potentially embarrassing interaction to hate himself for later.

"Hey, Beckett. You got a minute? I want to ask you about that trafficking case, but it can wait if—"

"Go ahead."

Gard was already regretting this decision, but he could hardly backup now. "Is a guy named Roger Hamilton part of it?"

Beckett's expression went from kind of distracted to focused in a second flat. "How'd you know that?"

Damn. "Look… I don't think this really connects, but…" He'd only ever told Laurel about Dani, and he wasn't too keen on sharing with Beckett, but… "The whole reason I was out at that place on Dry Road is because my sister had that address on her computer, and she's missing."

"Missing—"

Gard held up a hand. "Not a missing persons case. She's a drug addict. It's not the first time she's up and disappeared for a while. And considering the amount of drug paraphernalia in that place, I have to assume that's why she was there. She told her old boss this Roger Hamilton guy offered her a better job—but chances are, she's just using again."

"Hamilton is the guy who used the address on his work application. He has some connections to the group Hardy is looking into, but…we don't have a direct connection between this house and the trafficking ring just yet. Or even Roger Hamilton and the trafficking. It's all little pieces that don't connect."

Which just further proved…this was about drugs. There was no bigger mystery at play.

"We can add your sister's name to the case and—"

"Laurel has all the info on my sister if you need it." Gard wanted to jump on the possibility Dani was wrapped up in something she hadn't chosen, but there was absolutely no evidence. Especially if she was texting apologies to Sammy. "Update me when you get the chance, but I should stay out of it."

Beckett nodded slowly. "Sure thing. Let me know if you hear anything that might point otherwise, though, huh?"

"Yeah, I will." Gard walked out of the room quickly, feeling…antsy and pissed off and just generally…*worried*. How could she be doing this again?

His cell rang, and he pulled it out of his pocket, hoping it was something he could just ignore.

But it was Lia.

He answered immediately, worried Sammy had done something like…burn the bakery down. "Everything okay?"

"Yeah, it's good," Lia said reassuringly. "Sammy and I went for a little drive, and I just thought that, if it's okay with you, I'd drop her off at your place since we're near Bent. I won't leave until you get home. There's just no point going all the way back to the bakery, unless—"

"No, that's fine. Everything's okay, right?"

"Yeah, everything is good. Promise."

And Gard's worry unclenched a little, because he trusted Lia's *promise*.

"Are you sure that's going to taste good?" Lia asked speculatively. Most of her kitchen talents were of the sugar-and-butter variety. She liked to bake. She liked dessert and dessert masquerading as breakfast.

But this complicated cheese sauce Sammy was attempting… This was why Lia didn't like to cook. Cheese on its own? Good. Cheese when you mixed it into weird configurations? Possibly not good. Sugar and butter baked together? Pretty much *always* good.

But Sammy gave her a sharp, disgusted look. Her eyes

were still a little puffy from the earlier crying jag, but she was much more back to herself.

"I had higher hopes for your palate, Lia."

Lia rolled her eyes. She was sitting at the kitchen table, which gave her a view of what Sammy was doing in the small kitchen on the other side of the counter. She felt awkward being in Gard's house without him here, but she wasn't leaving the teen alone. And Sammy didn't seem to *want* to be alone.

So Lia sat at the table, hands in her lap, trying not to look around and study every inch of Gard's house. She couldn't say it had a ton of personality to make determinations about. The colors were nice, maybe a little matchy-matchy. The walls were pretty bare, but everything was… cozy. Despite the lack of decor, it did feel like someone really *lived* here.

The doorknob jiggled and Lia sat up straighter, nerves suddenly battling around for purchase. *Why* hadn't she just driven back to the bakery? Sure, it would have tacked on driving time for everyone, but…

The door opened and Gard stepped inside, wearing that damn uniform that was supposed to be an immediate turn-off. His hair was a little mussed, which was when she realized it was getting a little long for him. It was even starting to kind of curl.

Their eyes met briefly. Gard smiled. Lia smiled.

Oh hell.

"Well, something smells…" He hesitated ever so briefly before he aimed that smile at Sammy. "…good."

He was a liar. It did *not* smell good. But Lia was happy to get out of Dodge without dealing with that.

"I better get going," she said brightly, making a move to grab her purse that she'd set on the coffee table.

But Gard stood in her way, and Sammy bustled in from the kitchen.

"You have to stay," Sammy said, pointing at the table. "There are three plates."

"Oh, I—"

"I'm afraid it's the law, and I am here to enforce the law." Gard grinned at her. "Let me go change and wash up. Be right back."

He disappeared down the hall and Lia didn't realize she'd watched him walk away until she looked back at the kitchen to find Sammy studying her.

Heat crept up her cheeks. What the hell was she doing? It was really getting to be too much. Complicated. Messy. But Sammy was bustling around the kitchen and Lia didn't want to hurt her feelings—even if she was afraid the ambitious cheese sauce was going to be a nightmare.

So she sat back down at the table a bit helplessly. Sammy had everything all set up before Gard returned. He was in casual clothes now—jeans, a sweatshirt. His hair was wet like he'd run through the shower.

He moved to the table, his hand drifting over Sammy's head as he moved to his seat. Just a casual, affectionate gesture that made Lia's heart feel too big for her chest.

That big soft heart is going to get very, very bruised if you're not careful, Lia.

Gard led the conversation, asking Sammy about her day. Sammy lied, bald-faced that everything at the bakery had been fine and uneventful. Lia kept her mouth shut. She wasn't sure covering for Sammy was the best course of action, but she wasn't sure it…wasn't. It wasn't like something had really happened or changed. Sammy had just… let some of her feelings out. Did Gard really need to know every detail of that?

But Gard was too observant not to realize something had changed between when he'd dropped her off in the morning—angry and yelling—and now, with her cheerfully making a…truly terrible dinner.

"This isn't half bad," Gard said with a smile that was *fake*.

Because the food wasn't half good either, but Lia dutifully choked down a few terrible bites, before Sammy sighed gustily.

"Okay, this sucks."

Gard laughed, the sound low and rich. "You'll get 'em next time, kid. Can't learn if you don't practice and experiment." Sammy shoved her plate away dejectedly as Gard got to his feet. "No worries. There's always backup."

Sammy sighed again, resting her chin on her palm and watching her uncle suspiciously as he moved into the kitchen. "Please don't say potpie."

Gard opened the freezer and gestured at a stack of freezer meals with a flourish. "*Potpie.*"

Clearly it was some kind of inside joke, because Sammy was trying very hard not to laugh. Even with her kitchen failure. Which was a relief.

"Don't let him feed us frozen potpies, Lia," Sammy said, with fake desperation. "You have to do something to save us all."

"Sometimes you gotta take the losses on the chin," Lia said, smiling at Sammy, who was clearly enjoying herself. Which was a huge win in Lia's book. She had expected the second fail of the day to end in more sobs and tears, but Sammy seemed…really okay.

It didn't take a genius to figure out why. It was the man currently heating up *potpies* in the microwave.

He served Lia first, and even though she didn't like potpie, particularly the frozen variety, she sat there and ate it. Well, even she couldn't choke down the peas, but she ate the rest, while Gard and Sammy talked.

Lia would have been happy to sit there and listen, which was often how she got through life, never really belonging anywhere. Even now, feeling like she *did* belong in Hope Town, it was easy to keep to herself. To maintain a kind of tough-girl outer shell, chat about business or the weather, not…herself.

But Gard and Sammy didn't let her hide in plain sight. They kept asking her opinion on things or trying to use her as some sort of tiebreaker vote when they were good-naturedly arguing about something.

It was nothing, and yet it felt…special that they would just fold her in. *Too* special. Because this was still…not hers. *They* were not hers. She was like…a tourist.

Eventually the vacation would be over.

And that thought made her want to cry a little bit, which was just ridiculous and an overreaction. So, since they were all done eating, Lia got to her feet. "Thank you for dinner. Just text me what days you and the girls want to come to the bakery this week," she said to Sammy, moving for her purse. "Otherwise, I'll see you Saturday."

"Okay, but can I have Sunday off? Gard talked to Sara-beth's mom last night and said I could go to her party."

Sammy's smile made Lia smile too as she shouldered her purse. She'd known all along Gard would let her go even if he didn't want to, but she was glad it didn't seem to have caused too much turmoil.

"Of course. And if it's okay with Gard, you can take Saturday off too."

"Are you sure?" Sammy asked, frowning a little.

"You're going to need to sleep in Saturday if you're

going to go to a sleepover. I hear not much sleeping is done at those types of things. You guys think about it. Let me know."

She opened the front door and let herself out with a little wave on the way.

Outside in the cold air Lia managed a full, deep breath and let it out. Okay, she had to set herself some ground rules about the Fairhursts. Like no more dinners at Gard's house. It was just too…cozy and intimate. Maybe a restaurant every once in a while, but *not* his cute little house.

She'd only taken a few steps down the drive when she heard the door open behind her and she turned to see Gard stepping out onto his porch.

Oh. No.

He smiled at her in the beam of the porch light. "I just want to make sure there's no damages from this morning I need to be paying off."

"No, nothing like that." Lia tried to smile but she was… nervous. Not about her day with Sammy. About *him*. "She just…needed a break from everything, so we drove around a little bit."

He took a few steps toward her. "Sorry if the Fairhurst circus hijacked your weekend."

"You didn't," she said earnestly, because the last thing she wanted him thinking was that her nerves were some indication that she didn't want Sammy in her life, or Sammy had done something wrong. This weekend she'd felt…involved and useful and like she mattered and that was…

It was *a lot*, because aside from what she'd built at Hope Town—the bakery, her friends, all important but fused to that past of hers—she'd never felt like she belonged.

Gard took another few steps toward her. "I'm grateful, Lia. And before you get that pinched look, I know you don't want me to be. It's not a transactional kind of grateful. I appreciate you."

She couldn't find words to respond to that, because it touched something deep inside of her. She thought about what Sammy had said about protecting herself, and Lia knew she was falling into the same trap. Letting things seem…good, hopeful. She'd get clobbered.

And what had she told Sammy about *not* protecting yourself so much from the bad stuff you didn't see any good? Shouldn't she take her own advice?

That advice suddenly felt *very* dangerous.

"I left her with you this morning an angry, bitter teen and came home to…well, Sammy."

He was awfully close now, and she should probably step back. Turn and walk away.

"I'm glad I could help. I like spending time with her. Even…angry, bitter teen time. She's just…great."

He nodded. "Horrible kitchen experiments and all."

"It really *was* terrible."

He chuckled, the sound kind of rumbling through her out on his driveway. Standing just a shade too close and wanting to lean into that.

She cleared her throat. "Thanks for dinner. I'm sure I'll see you some day this week." She would have taken a step back, but his next words stopped her in her tracks.

"I liked coming home and seeing you in my house."

Oh *God*, that wasn't fair. Especially the way he said it. All low and…intimate.

He reached out, his hand—big and warm and calloused—touched her cheek. "You do something to me, Lia Blair. I haven't quite figured out what."

Maybe that was why she didn't know how to stop this. Because he did something to her too, and she was just as in the dark about what it was. What she was supposed to do about it.

Then he lowered his mouth to hers, pausing a breath away from actually touching, like he was waiting for her to tell him not to.

She should absolutely do that. Just explain it wasn't a good idea. But her heart was an echoing drumbeat in her ears, her body some other entity her rational thoughts didn't have control of. Because she mounted no objections, and leaned into the warmth radiating off of him.

And then his mouth was on hers. The kiss was gentle, but not exactly *chaste*. The only word she could come up with was…some kind of exploration. She could *feel* a subtle wave of warmth sweep through her muscles, one by one, until she'd completely relaxed into him.

She thought she might have been able to stay right here forever, the slow, thudding beat of her heart a perfect soundtrack to the best kiss of her life, by *far*.

But he eased his mouth away, those direct blue eyes right on hers when she managed to blink hers open. She was pretty sure her skin was *vibrating*. Had anyone ever kissed her like that? Made her feel like some imperative part of…everything.

His thumb grazed along her jaw, his other fingers resting gently against her neck. "Have you decided about dinner on Saturday?"

This was…probably not the best line to be walking. She had secrets she could probably never share with him. He was a *police officer*. Could he possibly understand all the twisted parts of her past even if she *could* tell him?

Which she couldn't.

But she did not tell him no. She did not pull away from

the warmth that seemed to radiate from his body or the directness in those blue eyes. She simply said, "Yes."

His mouth curved, that hand still on her face, his thumb moving up and down her jawline. A soft caress she couldn't possibly step away from. No one touched her, certainly not like she was special, desirable, interesting.

"Is that a yes you've been thinking about it, or a yes you'll go?"

Here was her out. Her chance to back off.

She didn't take it. "Both."

"I'm dropping Sammy off at the Thompsons' at five. I'll…pick you up at six?"

Lia nodded. She didn't trust her voice. She didn't trust *herself.*

"Then it's a date."

A date. Lia swallowed and then nodded. "Night, Gard." She had to force herself to turn and walk for her car. The air around her suddenly cold so she shivered. She slid into the car, let out a slow breath, then steeled herself for one last look.

He was standing on his porch again, hands deep in his pockets, watching her go. He lifted his hand in a wave, so Lia did the same, wondering what the *hell* she thought she was doing.

Apparently she was dating Corporal Gard Fairhurst, and even knowing that it could only lead to some terrible mistake, she couldn't stop the grin from spreading across her face as she drove home.

Chapter Ten

Dani didn't text Sammy again, and Gard kept his nose out of the trafficking case. Sammy was a little moody over the course of the week, but spending last Sunday with Lia had certainly evened out some of her reaction to Dani's text.

So they made it through the week without any big incidents. A little bit on eggshells, but they made it.

He'd managed to sneak one measly kiss out of Lia in the process of dropping Sammy off or picking her up over that time. A shame, but he'd have her to himself tonight.

Once he got through a few of the stipulations he'd set out in letting Sammy go to this party. Like he would drive her out there and see the house and meet Sarabeth's parents for himself.

Sammy complained about this stipulation bitterly as he drove out to Wilde, and then beyond. But she bounced in her seat, as excited as any elementary schooler heading to a birthday party.

Even though worry had wrapped around his lungs, and he probably wouldn't be able to take a full breath until he picked her up tomorrow morning, he smiled. Sammy was happy, and after last weekend? That was big.

The Thompson place was a big house. Old, but looked like a lot of work had been done to it lately. Still, it was out past the Wilde town limits—and Wilde was hardly a bustling metropolis. Gard couldn't decide if middle of nowhere was good—what could the kids get up to way out here? Or bad—what *couldn't* the kids get up to way out here?

The problem was, he'd spent over ten years dealing with *all* the trouble kids could get up to in Bent County—in town or out of it.

Gard pulled the truck to a stop in the big gravel drive in front of the Thompson house and killed the engine. He opened his door.

"Gard, you can't embarrass me like this," Sammy hissed as he moved to get out of his truck.

"I just want to meet Sarabeth's parents in person. That's the deal."

"It's *so* cringe."

Gard was hardly worried about being *cringe*. There were two adults standing near the porch, while teenagers seemed to roam the yard. Gard made a beeline for the woman with a slight baby bump and a man who Gard would have clocked as military from a mile away.

Sarabeth was holding court in front of a couple teenagers in the yard—wearing what looked like some kind of princess crown and eye black like she was getting ready to play softball or baseball. Gard really *was* glad Sammy had a friend who was so unapologetically herself, because he wanted that for Sammy.

Didn't mean that girl didn't scare the hell out of him. But for now, he focused on the adults. Sammy trudged behind him, still muttering about how *cringe* he was.

"Mrs. Thompson?"

The woman smiled at him and held out a hand. "Call me Jessie. This is my husband, Henry. You must be Sammy's Uncle Gard."

Gard shook both their hands. "This is a nice place you've got here."

"Thanks. We've put a lot of work into it," Henry said.

"Sammy!" Sarabeth called from across the yard, waving wildly. "Come over here."

Sammy sent Gard a questioning look and he gave her a little nod. She was clearly reluctant to leave him with the adults in case he was *too cringe*, but eventually she gave in and walked over toward Sammy and her group.

Gard turned his attention back to Jessie and Henry. "I'm not trying to be…" He didn't even know the right word. Obsessive? Overprotective? "I'm kind of new to being the guardian of a teenage girl. I've been told by the teenage contingency I might be overstepping."

Jessie smiled kindly. "We try not to be *too* overprotective here because Sarabeth *is* growing up, but…" Jessie began.

"But we fail. Consistently," Henry finished for his wife. "I'd keep her locked in the house if I thought it'd do any good," he grumbled, gesturing at Sarabeth.

Gard figured he might like this guy.

"This is the first time we've let Sarabeth have a party like this," Jessie said with a little sigh. "Usually we just do family, or just Izzy, but it's her sweet sixteen and…" Jessie shrugged, one hand resting on her bump. "There's going to be adult supervision at all times—we've got four adults to make sure the kids don't go sneaking off. No alcohol on the premises. Guns are locked in a safe where the kids won't be. The boys leave at ten sharp, and Henry or Dunne—that's my brother-in-law—will drive them home if their parents *forget* to pick them up. So no chance for stragglers."

Gard couldn't find fault with any of it, and he'd been… well, maybe hoping to. "Sounds like you've got it all figured out," he said, trying to sound polite and not frustrated.

"Sarabeth has let me in on a little bit about Sammy's background," Jessie told him gently. "There's a reason Sarabeth and Izzy get along so well. They understand each other. They've had it rough, and I get the impression Sammy has too and that's why they've folded her into their little group so easily. We'll take good care of her. I promise."

Gard knew he'd still worry, but at least he'd have a better chance of convincing himself it was *pointless* worry.

He thanked the Thompsons for having Sammy. He wanted to go say goodbye to Sammy and lecture her about manners and safety, but she was laughing with Sarabeth and she looked…

Happy. Without a care in the world. Like a fifteen-year-old should. Like *he'd* been able to be. And Dani hadn't, because even then she'd been set up with impossible expectations. He knew Dani didn't want that for Sammy, and he didn't either.

He got in his truck, then pulled out his phone and sent off a quick text: Be good. Be polite. Then, he quickly tacked on: Have fun. Love you.

After a minute, she sent him a series of emojis. Including the vomit one.

But also a heart.

So he drove away from the Thompson house, still worried and nervous, but with a smile on his face. And when he drove past the gravel turnoff to Dry Road, he didn't turn onto it to check out a certain abandoned house.

He wanted to.

But he drove on.

After all, he had a date.

"Why the hell am I doing this?" Lia demanded of her two friends as she stood half dressed in her bedroom. She'd enlisted their help since she hadn't been on a date in—maybe a decade. And those *dates*, looking back, hadn't exactly been normal.

"Beats me," Albennie said, so unhelpfully, sprawled out on Lia's bed while Franny rummaged around in Lia's closet.

"Because Gard is nice and good-looking and you like him," Franny said, sending Albennie a somewhat disapproving glare.

"You're just saying that because of Royal," Albennie accused, mentioning Franny's boyfriend, who worked as a deputy at Bent County.

"And Royal would know that Gard is a good guy, since Gard trained him and they're friends." Franny appeared from the closet with two clothing items hanging from hangers. "You could wear this dress with a sweater over it." She overlaid them so Lia could see the vision.

Lia bit her lip. "We're just going to Fairmont."

"It's hardly a ball gown, Lia," Albennie said disgustedly. "It's cute and casual and the perfect first-date outfit."

It was Albennie's no-nonsense approval of the outfit that had Lia taking it and moving into the bathroom and putting it on. She'd already done her hair and makeup. Nothing fancy. Just a little color on her face and actually letting her hair down—something she never did just because baking required it back and out of her face, and she'd gotten used to pinning it back every day.

When she returned to her room, Franny clasped her hands together and studied Lia critically.

"You look perfect," she declared.

Lia tried to smile at the compliment, but her mouth felt stiff and weird.

Franny slung an arm over her shoulders and gave a squeeze. "I've never seen you nervous like this. It's so cute."

"She's nervous with the kid too, so the wedding bells are a little misplaced. The Fairhursts just make her jumpy."

Franny scowled at Albennie. "Why do you hate romance?"

"Because men suck?"

"I know plenty of men who don't suck," Franny replied loftily.

"Yeah, *and* plenty of men who *do*."

"Gard doesn't suck." Lia studied herself in the full-length mirror on her closet door. She was worried it was a little too fussy, but it wasn't bad. When she glanced at her suddenly quiet friends, they were both studying her with questioning gazes.

"What?"

"You've got it *bad* for someone going on a first date," Albennie said, but she didn't sound dismissive like she had been.

"I don't know that it's a first date exactly. I've had dinner with him a few times. Sammy's been there, so it wasn't like an official date, but still it was…kind of."

"It doesn't count unless he kissed you afterward," Franny said.

Lia remained silent, trying to decide what pair of shoes to wear, and decidedly not commenting on *that*.

"He kissed you *already*?" Franny demanded.

Lia didn't meet her gaze. "Maybe."

"Well, this changes everything," Albennie said, apparently interested *now*. "Describe the when, where, how, and why."

"Um, *no*."

"Why not?"

"Because that's…private."

"That good, huh?" Albennie said with a grin that Lia couldn't quite help returning. *Good* didn't begin to cover it.

"So this isn't a first date. It's not even a second date with that smug look over a kiss," Franny said, looking around Lia's room in dismay. "We should probably clean up your room."

"Why?"

"Well, you might want to…" Franny trailed off, gesturing at Lia's bed.

Heat crept into Lia's cheeks. She hadn't even considered…that. Not in any *concrete* way. Because this *was* a first date, even if it…kind of wasn't. "That's moving faster than I…move."

"I'd speed up for a guy who looks like that, considering I've *never* seen you with a guy," Albennie muttered. "How long has it been?"

Lia was not about to touch that subject with a ten-foot pole.

"We better go," Franny said, glancing at the clock with some worry. "We don't want to ambush him."

"Speak for yourself," Albennie replied.

Franny shook her head and grabbed Albennie's arm and started dragging her out of Lia's room. Lia trailed after them, suddenly about ten times more nervous than she already had been.

Why had she agreed to a date? Why did she think this was a good idea? Why—

The sound of an engine when Franny opened the door had them all peering outside. Gard's truck was pulling in.

"Behave," Lia heard Franny mutter to Albennie as Gard turned off the truck and got out. He was wearing dark slacks and a button-up shirt that accentuated the broad strength in his shoulders. He was so classically handsome it didn't seem fair or real that he was also just…such a good guy.

"Hey, Franny. Albennie." He greeted her friends as they passed—him moving toward the door where Lia stood and them heading for Franny's car.

"Hi, Gard," Franny said brightly, still dragging Albennie along. "We were just leaving. You two have fun!"

Gard looked past the duo to Lia. His smile deepened as he made his way up her walk.

Lia's heart was in a full-on gallop now. She was nothing but a sack of nerves, but they weren't questioning why she'd agreed to this.

That *smile* was why.

When he made it to where she stood in her doorway, he reached out, wrapped a tendril of hair around his finger. "I've never seen your hair down before." He flashed that lethal grin at her. "Wow."

All she could seem to think was… Maybe she *should* have cleaned up her room.

Chapter Eleven

Gard helped Lia into his truck and then they started to drive out to Fairmont. Lia asked how dropping off Sammy at the party had gone, and Gard asked about her day at the bakery. Conversation was easy, even if there was a strange layer of nerves over it.

He didn't generally get nervous about dates, but it was easy to realize why he was in this moment.

Gard had never really entertained serious before. He realized in this moment that even when he'd been a kid, there'd always been something *else* that required his attention—good grades, getting into law school, then Dani and Sammy. Even when Dani had her life together, his demanding, ever-changing work schedule that sometimes required overtime at the drop of the hat often caused relationships to peter out.

Dating was easy. Relationships weren't. Particularly when he devoted so much time to his job *and* Dani and Sammy.

Lia was hardly just a date. And still, somehow everything felt easy with her. Even working around Sammy's schedule. It wasn't like Lia was some separate part to be added on top of everything else. It was like she slotted right in.

Gard could admit it wasn't the most *comfortable* realization. If he thought too hard on it, he got a little nervous. Like every little step with Lia was stamping his future in stone.

But that was silly. Life was full of choices—including ones that could change everything at the drop of the hat. He knew that better than most. There was no avoiding it. Choices came at you whether you wanted them to or not.

Besides, he hadn't been lying about the *wow*. Sure, Lia always looked pretty. He'd been attracted to her from the start, but her hair down softened…something. It added to this layer of vulnerable he'd seen under that tough outer mask she wore.

Maybe there was something twisted in him, but he liked the dichotomy. He thought it spoke to courage. He respected the hell out of courage.

The restaurant wasn't upscale exactly—he didn't think Lia would have been comfortable with that any more than he would be—but it was a few steps up from HJs.

She sat across from him in the dim light, studying the menu. "Sammy told me she was disappointed in my palate. Which made me think I should try something new, but…"

"Have you been having nightmares about the cheese sauce like I have?"

She laughed, grinning up at him over her menu. "That *and* the peas in the potpie. They might be my two food archnemeses."

"Peas and bad cheese sauce. Mushrooms and fishy pizza toppings. Got it."

Her grin faded a little bit, but not in a bad way. Like she was surprised he remembered what she'd said at the pizza place about what toppings she liked.

Which hadn't even been a conscious choice. Just like he'd been telling himself before. Lia just…slotted right in.

They ordered and settled into an easy conversation that mostly revolved around Sammy. Her interests at the bakery. And the things she *wasn't* interested in. Like cleaning. Gard didn't mind focusing on Sammy to ease their way in, but it meant he wasn't quite expecting it when Lia changed the subject.

"Why did you decide not to go to law school?" she asked, like that was a question that had been sitting in her head since Sammy had told her about it last weekend. "Was it because of Sammy?"

Gard considered. He knew all the reasons. He'd had to mine them in family therapy. But he wasn't always sure he knew how to articulate them. "Yes, but not quite in the way you mean. It wasn't just to…support them. It was a choice I made for me too."

"You didn't want to be a lawyer?"

"I'm honestly not sure. It was just always a given. Dad's a lawyer. Grandpa's a judge. Great-Grandpa was a lawyer, judge, *and* state senator. And so on. So it was just always… expected. I probably would have been good at it. I might have even liked it, but…more than what I liked or would have been good at, Dani getting pregnant was the turning point of me realizing I needed to do something on my own. Without the Fairhurst name or Dad's interference."

"You said Dani was good at debate. Was she planning on law school too?"

Gard shook his head. "No. There were expectations for Dani too, but…well, they were different for the *female* Fairhurst. Her role wasn't to *be* anybody. It was to look perfect and find the right husband."

Lia got a little still at that, so he hurried on so she didn't think *he* subscribed to that way of thinking.

"Even back then, I thought they were a little old-fashioned, but I was also young and selfish and thought Dani was…overreacting when she complained about the difference. Being a baby or a girl or whatever insult worked. When she'd complain about that stuff, I didn't really listen. My life was just fine, you know."

Lia nodded, but of course she didn't know. She'd run away from home at fifteen. A story he really wanted to hear. Which probably meant laying his out there. It was only fair.

"Dani always…rebelled against their expectations, but it got pretty bad in high school. I was off at college in Michigan. I didn't consider what she was doing addiction-wise then. So she drank socially and underage? I had. The pot was a little bit of a concern, but I just figured she was trying to shock our parents. And I knew me telling her not to wasn't going to accomplish anything. I thought she'd… grow out of it."

It still sat with the weight of guilt that he'd been so… self-absorbed. That he hadn't answered Dani's calls for help until…

"When she found out she was pregnant, I was the first person she told. Well, aside from the asshole boyfriend of hers. She wanted to run away but needed help. I sure as hell didn't know what to do, but I really thought running away wasn't the answer. So, I convinced her to tell our parents. We planned it for when I was home on break, so I could go with her. I knew they'd be furious, but I thought… I really thought *I* could reason with them. Maybe they wouldn't listen to her, but they always listened to me."

"But not this time?"

He shook his head. "They gave her two choices. Have an abortion or never step foot in their home again."

Lia's breath caught, clearly commiserating with Dani. So Gard kept going.

"They were so…cold in that moment. Here Dani was, crying and scared and just…a kid. And they were treating her like an employee who'd stolen from them." Gard shook his head. "It was like watching their masks get stripped off in real time. All these things I'd never paid attention to, never poked at, just let slide… I couldn't pretend anymore for the sake of peace or ease or whatever."

He blew out a breath. He supposed it was heavy stuff for a first date, but these weren't exactly normal first-date protocols when Lia had been wrapped up in his and Sammy's life for the past two months now.

"After that, I told Dani I was going to take care of everything. Because she *was* young and scared. She needed someone to be an adult. I didn't decide not to go to law school in the fall just because I couldn't really help Dani if I was in school. It was bigger than that. My parents' behavior in that moment opened my eyes to who they really were and who I would be if I followed the plan they set out for me. It was like wearing blinders my whole life and having them ripped off. I wanted to be there for Dani, but more… I didn't want to be the kind of man who let his sister suffer because he'd had it all right. Who fell in line with parents who could be so cruel to their own daughter."

"So from there on out it was you and Dani against the world?"

"Pretty much. Even that… It was all easier on me. The police academy was a good fit. Challenging, but it felt… right. After Sammy was born, Dani suffered from postpartum depression, and we didn't really have the resources to know what that was at the time. I was busy trying to get through the academy, so when she fell into harder drugs… Well, it was just a tough time. I got her into rehab about the time I got my job at county."

"It seems to fit you. Police work, that is. Franny said Royal says you're great. Do you—"

He could see she was letting him off the hook from having to get too deep into Dani's drug addiction, but he wasn't about to keep talking about himself. Not when he knew she had stories of her own.

"Before we get into my job, it's your turn."

"My turn for what?"

"To tell me your story. Why'd you run away and never go back?"

LIA BLINKED AT HIM. She'd been so wrapped up in his story—his *honesty*—she hadn't prepared herself for the turnaround.

She should have. She should have been protecting herself, because she couldn't be as honest as he was being. Of course, she'd given Sammy pieces of her childhood, hadn't she? She could give him *those* pieces at least.

The hard part was…actually *wanting* to give him the whole. He'd been so open and honest—she knew, because he hadn't painted himself as Dani's savior. She could see the way he felt guilty, even if he shouldn't, for being a bit of a self-absorbed brother before Dani had gotten pregnant.

But he'd stepped up when he'd realized. And for Sammy's whole life, he'd been there. Being the hero, whether he saw it that way or not. Lia did, and she knew Sammy did too—even when she was mad at him and not wanting to be grateful for him.

So, even though it gave her pause, Lia told him what she'd told Sammy. About never really knowing her parents because of their drug problem. How she'd been raised mostly by her aunt and uncle. But since Gard knew she had run away, and he wasn't a vulnerable teen she was afraid of influencing, she figured she could give him a few details into that too.

"My aunt and uncle didn't like me. I think every year I didn't turn into the perfect obedient robot, they hated me a little more. I don't know that if I'd been their biological daughter they would have felt that way, but I was tainted. I was a burden, and they were the type of people who thought burdens should pay the person who shouldered them back. I did not subscribe to that belief. Defiantly."

"Good," he said emphatically, reaching across the table and putting his big hand over hers. He had a scar across two knuckles. There was something about that scar, his story, hers, this moment that seemed to work together to offer her a few realizations.

One, her first and immediate dislike of him had been born out of this feeling right here. A warm, excited unfurling. Like she'd seen him and recognized something in him would…be a threat to the very careful, distant life she'd built in Hope Town.

The second realization was that she'd been distant not because of her secrets so much as because… She really didn't think anyone would ever be able to see beyond who she'd been or what she'd done. But if anything, Gard's story about how he'd come to open his eyes to his family was such a clear indicator that he'd…give her a lot of grace.

Which of course, made her even guiltier that she couldn't share it.

"You don't have to finish the story, Lia." He squeezed her hand. His smile was kind.

She hated it.

"No, it's okay." She would tell him what she could. She made a promise to herself to always tell him what she could.

The waitress came by with the dessert they'd ordered,

and one more glass of wine, and Lia steeled herself to tell a portion of the story. A portion that hopefully was enough for Gard to feel like she wasn't…holding back.

"I'm not sure I would have run away all on my own. I had this friend. I was a freshman. She was a senior. I look back and realize she…probably had worse problems at home than I did, but we commiserated about that. She was planning to run away after graduation. She'd met some guy who claimed he could give her a great job in California and I just…begged her to let me come with her. So I did. And I never looked back."

And that was about all she could tell him. Even though she could read the questions in his blue eyes. Even though she thought maybe he'd…actually understand.

"So even now, you've never contacted your aunt and uncle? You just…stayed away forever?"

"For all they know, I'm dead," Lia said, knowing she sounded flat and perhaps a little bitter. "I assume they hope I am. I hated them, so I didn't care what they thought."

"Past tense?"

Lia really sat with that question for a moment, sipped her wine. "No, I still hate them. I'm just not sure it's the healthiest feeling so I *try* not to. In their warped way, they tried. They never treated me like theirs, but I still went to the private school their kids went to, and those damn etiquette classes."

"Private school and etiquette classes," Gard echoed. "You've been holding out on me." He pointed a fork in her direction. "Lia Blair was raised with money."

He was lightening the moment, and it made her smile in spite of herself. "Charity money, it was made very clear. Although if I had been a fine, upstanding ward they might have happily used me to marry someone who could give them better social standing or whatever the hell it was they wanted. But I just…couldn't be that. I wouldn't even answer to my full name they insisted on using."

Which was the wrong thing to say. A slipup of…too much real.

"And what is your full name?" he demanded. "Please tell me it's as stuffy as Gardner Elliot Fairhurst the *Fourth*."

She didn't have a clue as to how he made her want to smile in this awful moment where she'd have to lie to him. She could hardly give her real, full name to a *cop*. No matter how hard she was falling for said cop.

Some of his amusement in his expression turned to concern when she didn't answer. "Did I strike a nerve?"

"No." Not the way he meant. She couldn't give him the real *real* name, but couldn't she at least…give him a little? Lia *was* the only part of her Hope Town name that was real-ish. So the full name of that couldn't be a mistake. "Cornelia."

He made a noise, kind of like a snort, but he tried to cover it with a cough.

"Are you *laughing* at my name?" she said, shocked at how bad he was hiding it.

"No! No, of course not. Cornelia is…" He covered his mouth, made another coughing sound—clearly meant to cover up a laugh. "It's a name."

He didn't even have a clue. Her *real* name was even more ridiculous. And for some insane reason, she wanted to tell him. She wanted to see him try to hide laughing at *that*.

What's the harm? He wouldn't know your real last name.

He cleared his throat, even with amusement dancing in his eyes, his expression was serious. "Okay, what's the middle name then?"

"Oh, no. I don't think so, Mr. Laughy."

"Come on. Cough it up. It can't be that bad."

She raised an eyebrow at him. It was a dare, and she couldn't resist a dare. "Edwina."

He just stared at her. "You're messing with me."

"I am not."

"Your name is Cornelia Edwina Blair?"

No, her name was Edwina Cornelia Pitt, but that was a hell of a lot closer than she had a right to be telling anyone. But Gard was grinning, and she just couldn't hold on to all the *shoulds*. "That's not nearly as stuffy as being a *fourth*."

"I beg to differ."

"That's only because you're a *fourth*," she replied, grinning at him. The waitress came by with the bill and Gard paid and they got up to leave.

They walked out, and Gard took her hand in his, entwining their fingers.

It just felt normal. Better than normal actually, because her life *could* be lonely, just as Sammy had once accused her of. It was a lonely of her own making, which meant sometimes it wasn't so bad, but Gard made it feel…

Well, like she wasn't all that interested in being alone.

They got in his truck, and he took her hand again, holding it the whole drive back to her house. They talked about the restaurant, their mutual fear of Sarabeth, and Gard told her about how he was thinking about getting Sammy a dog for her birthday in the spring but was worried neither of them really had the time for it.

When he pulled into her driveway, he let her hand go and pushed the truck into Park. But he didn't turn off the ignition. He just turned toward her.

"Well, I didn't track Sammy's phone for hours, and I have you to thank."

She chuckled at that. "Any chance that lasts through the night?"

"Not a one. The second you're inside, I'm making sure she's where she's supposed to be."

Maybe she shouldn't laugh at that, but he just…cared so much. She wondered how her teenage years might have been different if anyone had cared about her even half as much.

She shook her head. No use going down that depressing road.

"I had a really nice time, Gard."

"Me too."

She hesitated for a second. She should get out of the truck, but wasn't he going to kiss her good-night? And at least—

His mouth touched hers before she could finish the thought. She sighed into the kiss. It was an awkward angle, leaning over the center console, but his lips made her forget about that. His fingers brushed down her neck and she shivered in response.

When he pulled back, she blinked up at him. That moment held for a second or two, making her sluggish heart pound hard against her ribs. Because it was a serious look, a serious moment, a heavy, kind of scary thing fluttering there in her chest.

He smiled at her, but his jaw was tight. "Night, Lia."

Kind of like a dismissal. Which was…a little weird, but maybe she was just misreading a sign or something.

"Night," she offered, not sure why she felt…off-kilter all of a sudden. She slid out of the truck and into the cold night. She huddled into her jacket and felt oddly…emotional.

The date had been great. The kiss had been great. The moment after… Well, certainly he'd felt it too. So maybe it had put *him* off-kilter. Maybe he wasn't looking for something that...*deep.*

Because he'd just said good-night. He hadn't mentioned doing it again.

Oh *God,* had she made some kind of fool at herself, but she was so bad at this she didn't even know it?

Halfway up her walk, she heard the engine cut out and the door slam shut. Then Gard's voice saying her name.

She turned back to face him. He was moving toward her, something like...intent written across his features.

Her heart leapt, her stomach clenched. *Uh oh.*

She didn't want to have to explain to him she wasn't quite ready for that step, but she was very afraid her body wouldn't *let* her explain it. Because when he got close, reached out, and pulled her to him, she just...let him.

He was so tall and broad, it was like being enveloped by a blanket straight out of the dryer. An immediate shock of heat against the cold night. Especially when his mouth dropped to hers—demanding and needy all at the same time.

She just...melted into it all. Forgetting everything else except the hard press of his body against hers. Her skin was vibrating again. *Everything* inside of her was vibrating.

He eased away, but his breath was as unsteady as hers. He looked at her like he was searching her face for something, but he didn't know what. "What do you do when the bakery is closed on Monday?" he asked.

Which was a...really weird segue she didn't fully understand, but she answered anyway. "If I have admin stuff I'm behind on, I do that. Or sometimes I just take the day off and relax."

"I don't work Mondays, and Sammy's got school. Why don't we go to lunch?"

"O-okay."

"Pick you up at noon?"

She nodded.

He released her and cold air rushed in between them. A reminder she…she had a lot of work to do before whatever came after a kiss like *that* was going to be acceptable.

"Good night, Gard," she said softly, stepping away from him.

"Night, Lia," he replied. He also took a step back, then moved for his truck. He got in, but he didn't drive away— and she knew he wouldn't until she was safely inside.

Where he could be too, if you invited him.

She shook that thought away as she stepped inside, locked the door behind her.

She wasn't quite ready for that step. Well, she *was*, but she needed to make a few choices about…honesty and what a future looked like when someone had secrets as big as hers.

But for the first time since she'd come to Hope Town all those years ago, young, traumatized, and scared… She really wanted to figure it out instead of hide from it.

Chapter Twelve

The sleepover had been a success. Sammy had ridden the high of that party for at least a week. She crashed down the next week when her science grade dipped and Gard had insisted she spend her Friday night working on the lab report she was allowed to redo instead of going to Sarabeth's softball game after school.

He'd received an epic cold shoulder for that one.

But then Lia had come out with them for Saturday dinner and Sammy seemed to even out again, excitedly regaling Lia with tales of her great debate club practice triumph, shutting up some pretentious senior with her *excellent* arguments—Sammy's words.

Lia just had a way about her with Sammy. Their situations weren't really alike. Maybe Sammy resented him sometimes, but she knew she was cared for and about. Lia clearly hadn't had that. Maybe ever.

And still she'd turned out…amazing. Smart and sweet and funny and kind.

Yeah, he had it bad, no doubt. He was surprised Sammy hadn't called him out on it. He'd catch her watching them sometimes, carefully cataloguing whatever teenagers noticed about *old people*—her words again—having a relationship. But she didn't say anything about it—except to always push him to include Lia in whatever their plans were. So he assumed that there was some kind of stamp of approval in there.

Gard was currently trying to figure out how to have another night alone with Lia. He didn't mind holding her hand or giving her a quick, casual kiss in front of Sammy, but that was about it, which left him a bit…frustrated when the only time he ever got her alone was in his driveway if he walked her out to her car, or for their standing Monday lunch date.

Of course, if he let Sammy hang out at Sarabeth's softball practice Friday after school and then go to a movie in Fairmont like the girls wanted to, he *would* have at least part of a night with Lia to himself.

But three unsupervised teenagers at a movie theater… was that really wise? Sure, he'd been doing that kind of thing at fifteen, but weren't times different?

Gard shook his head. Not the time to be going over that again. He was at *work*. He'd been trying to finish this report for too long already. He needed to focus on *it*, not his personal life.

He looked at the computer screen. The inane details he had to put into the system over some found bicycle that no one had reported missing, but he had to log as found property anyway. A particularly annoying waste of time.

He stared at the screen, typed one word before his focus wandered again. He pulled his phone out of his pocket and opened up a text to Lia.

You free Friday night? Sammy's going to the movies with the girls. Because didn't Sammy deserve some normal? And didn't he?

Yes.

He started typing out a message about maybe going to a

movie—not the *same* movie as the girls, but if they were all in the same *theater*, that wasn't being *too* overprotective, was it?

But a message from Lia came in before he could finish.

Do you want to come over to my house? I'll make us dinner.

He stared at that brief message. His immediate internal response was: *Hell yes*. But that meant letting Sammy go to this movie on her own.

And if he let her do that, it meant dinner. At Lia's. He was desperately curious what that might entail. He hadn't really seen the inside of her house before.

He could see that she was typing and quickly typed his own response before she took her offer back. Yes.

"You got a minute?"

Gard nearly dropped his phone at Detective Beckett's voice. He'd been so wrapped up in the text conversation he hadn't heard anyone come into the room.

Gard cleared his throat, tried to look casual as he put his phone down on the table. "Sure."

Beckett raised an eyebrow, but he didn't question it. "I've got a picture I'd like you to take a look at." He set the laptop he was carrying on the table Gard was sitting at.

Gard peered at the picture on the screen and his stomach dropped as Beckett pointed to the woman standing off to the side of what appeared to be a still from security footage.

"Laurel said this looks a lot like your sister," Beckett said.

Gard had to work hard to make sure his voice was devoid of any kind of emotion. "That's her." And just like that, any good feelings he'd had about today were completely gone.

There was no *good* reason Dani was in a picture Beckett was showing him.

"You're sure?"

Gard gave a sharp nod. "Where is this?"

"A warehouse outside of Hardy. A Bent County deputy witnessed a drug deal going down. Intervened. He was on his own, so only managed to arrest the buyer. We're trying to identify all the players. Investigate."

"Well, Laurel's right about that ID. Dani Fairhurst. No doubt. I don't know the guys."

Beckett nodded. "And you don't have any idea where your sister is staying?"

Gard thought about the address on her computer, but no one had been living there. No doubt she'd been there, done drugs there, but she wasn't staying there. "No."

"Not going to be awkward if I have to arrest your sister, is it?"

Gard sighed. "No. Just life." Gard tried to keep his tone even, but it was a hard-won thing. "So, she wasn't selling?"

Beckett shook his head. "Didn't look like it from Stanley's body cam footage. Just hanging out with the seller."

And Gard's experience with Dani and drugs was just complicated enough to feel *some* relief over the fact she was just a bystander. When being a bystander wasn't much better at all.

"Look. This case is mainly Hardy's, and I can let them handle it and her if you want to keep this separate," Beckett said, a certain softness to his tone that hadn't been there before. Or maybe ever. "Or I can wade in and take over the part that deals with her. Take a softer approach, if that'd be better for you."

It was…a kindness. Gard knew he should take it, no

questions asked, but… "Not exactly known for your soft touch, Beckett."

He snorted. "No. But I'm getting married next month. According to my future sister-in-law, it's turned me into a big softy."

Gard wanted to be amused by that, but he couldn't find any levity. "I'd appreciate it then. Look… I know what this is going to sound like. But she's no hardened criminal. She's got a drug problem, and I'm not saying she hasn't broken any laws, or that you shouldn't arrest her if she has. But she's… She tries. For her kid. She just can't resist that addiction. Any way this can be a little soft on her, I'd be appreciative."

"Got it." Beckett picked up the laptop.

But as some of those details meshed in Gard's head, he had more questions. "I thought you were helping the Hardy cops with a human trafficking case? What's that got to do with a drug dealer?"

Beckett nodded. "Yeah. It all connects, or at least we're trying to prove it does. We've got some names, some theories, and they all connect to that address on Dry Road. That's technically unincorporated Bent County, so we've got the jurisdiction on that, but most of the players are in Hardy."

Connects.

"Can you email me that picture?"

Beckett hesitated, then shrugged. "Yeah, I guess that'd be okay. I'll send it over in a minute."

Gard tapped his fingers against his desk. Grasping at straws again. She'd looked just fine in that picture, hadn't she? Standing next to a drug dealer. Hardly the first time. Even if that *was* mixed up in some human trafficking group, it didn't mean Dani was being held against her will. Clearly she wasn't.

But when his email pinged with the picture, *and* the body cam footage, Gard set aside the work he should be doing and studied both.

Coming to no conclusions except that this nagging feeling of *missing something* wasn't his gut, just wishful thinking.

Wishful thinking only ever hurt Sammy. It never solved any problems. So he had to set it aside and away. And hope that whatever Beckett's investigation found, it was soon, and got Dani off the streets.

LIA STOOD OUTSIDE the Simmonses' house with nerves battling around in her stomach. She didn't know exactly what she was hoping to get out of this. She just knew…

She couldn't keep holding parts of herself back from Gard. And she couldn't put anyone in Hope Town in danger by telling him about her past.

Which left her sitting between a rock and a hard place.

And Lia was used to dealing with her own rocks and hard places, but… Ever since her first real date with Gard, she had been trying to decide what to do, how to approach this. She didn't have the answers when it came to Gard, couldn't find them.

Which meant she needed help. Something she was definitely not used to asking for.

But tonight, Gard was coming over to her house for dinner. The girls were going to a movie after Sarabeth's softball practice. Izzy's stepmom was driving them to the theater, and Sarabeth's stepdad was going to pick them up and drop them off at their respective houses.

Thinking about *step*parents left Lia feeling awkward because… Because it was just too damn easy to think about a future that was…permanent like that. Where she'd be included and—

You haven't even slept with him yet.

Hence why she'd offered to cook dinner for them tonight instead of go out when he'd told her about Sammy's plans.

A home-cooked meal in her house had connotations. She was hoping it did, anyway.

And she had to get this talk with Zach over with so she could go home and finish making that dinner. She would have talked to Zach earlier in the week, but he and his family had been out of town.

And she'd maybe still been hoping to figure things out on her own. No help needed. Just relying on Lia Blair, the person she was these days.

But time had run out, and the only answers she was going to find required help.

Steeling herself, Lia knocked on the door.

Lucy was the one who opened it, dressed casually in jeans and an oversized sweatshirt, her hair pulled back haphazardly. She looked every inch a frazzled mom of young kids and nothing like her bad-girl country singer persona.

It still struck Lia sometimes that Zach's sharp, funny wife was *the* Daisy Delaney, but Lucy did a pretty great job of blending.

"Lia," Lucy greeted with a friendly smile. "Zach'll be down in a sec. Come on in."

Lia nodded, trying to force a smile. "Thanks."

Lucy nodded, leading Lia through the house. Toys were strewn through the living room, and a baby monitor sat on the coffee table, the green light on. "Kids asleep?" Lia asked, hoping conversation would keep her nerves at bay.

Lucy nodded. "Well, Rylie is. Coop is having quiet play-time."

As if on cue, a muffled sound came out of the baby monitor, kind of like a roar.

Lucy rolled her eyes. "I thought I'd finally ushered us out of the dino fad, and what does my brother do when we visit? Takes us to a museum with dinosaur bones. Now, we're back."

"It was a nice visit?"

"Yeah, it was. So, is this meeting with Zach an office meeting or a living room meeting?"

Lia tried to keep her smile in place, but it faltered. Lucy took her by the arm, gave her a reassuring squeeze. "Office it is." Lucy led her through the dining room and back into Zach's office. "Make yourself comfortable. I'll go see what's taking him so long."

Lia nodded and forced herself to sit in the chair opposite Zach's desk.

Zach Simmons had created Hope Town. He owned all the buildings, financed all the businesses on startup. A former FBI agent, he'd created a security business *and* a down-low privatized WitSec program for women like Lia.

So Lia had been in his office quite a few times over the past seven years of her being here. At first, for updates on the people she'd helped put behind bars. Then for meetings about the bakery or Hope Town in general. As one of the first residents of Zach Simmons's Hope Town, she'd been in at the ground floor. She and Lane Webb, who ran the antique store. They'd grown with Hope Town, had a say in what that growth looked like.

But Zach was the leader, the man in charge. When Albennie had been kidnapped this summer, he was the one who'd stepped in and dealt with the FBI, local law enforcement, and even been part of bringing in Royal to keep Franny safe—since she'd been a witness to the kidnapping.

Zach was the one who facilitated keeping all the women of Hope Town safe.

Zach strode into the office. "Sorry to hold you up, Lia."

"I'm sorry if I'm interrupting your afternoon. You guys just got back and…"

He waved it away. "No worries. So, what can I do for you?" He sat down behind his desk, impressive computer equipment all around him. The…breadth of what he did for all of them seemed to land on her shoulders like a ton of bricks and all the careful words Lia had planned just… disappeared.

Was she really going to sit here and ask this guy if she was allowed to spill all her past secrets to the guy she was dating? Wasn't that a *her* decision?

She thought of the fear she'd felt when Albennie had been kidnapped, all because of a leak from someone who'd worked on the case that had led Albennie here. Things Albennie still hadn't disclosed to her, and probably never would.

No matter how close you got in Hope Town, there were no-go zones. Did she really think she had any right to plow into these accepted no-go zones?

No, it just…wasn't her choice to make. Not when danger could come calling and have real consequences.

"Everything okay?" Zach asked when she said nothing.

Lia fidgeted in her seat. "Sorry. This is…awkward."

Zach merely raised an eyebrow. Lia had to inwardly give herself a shake to focus and just…deal. She wanted a real life. She wanted her friends safe. So she was going to have to wade into some awkward areas.

"It's just… I know being a part of Hope Town comes with certain rules. About keeping our pasts secret. That's always been pretty easy because most of the people I associate with have pasts they're keeping a secret too."

Zach nodded along. "And that's…changed?"

"I'm…seeing someone." God, that sounded lame. "He's a cop. You probably know him. That's not the point." *Focus, Lia.* "The point is, I feel like I can't keep my whole past this big secret. It's getting in the way of living my life, but I certainly don't want to… I don't want to jeopardize anything in Hope Town just because I want to tell someone about what led me here."

"So you want…my permission?" Zach asked carefully. "To tell this cop you're seeing about what landed you in Hope Town?"

Lia inhaled against shaky nerves. "You run this program, Zach. It's your town. It's your rules. It's…yours. With everything that happened to Albennie this summer, how can I just…" She sucked in a breath. This wasn't the planned speech. She needed to focus on the planned speech. "Yes, I want to tell him about my past and how I ended up here. I know that isn't part of the Hope Town deal, so I wanted to talk it through with you first. I can't quit the bakery, so—"

"No one is going to ask you to quit the bakery just because you want to tell someone about yourself," Zach said firmly. "But…" Zach was quiet for a long time, but it was a soft kind of a quiet. A thinking quiet. He breathed deeply before speaking, and when he did speak, his voice was gentle.

"You didn't sign a contract or a vow of secrecy. You just came here to be safe. I can tell you that the Corbins are all still in jail. I'll be notified if that even has a chance of changing, and of course, I'd let you know right away."

It was why traditional WitSec wouldn't take her—the people she'd testified against were in jail. But the FBI agent she'd helped to bring down the Corbin family had been worried about retribution from some lower-level parts of the trafficking ring Lia had unwittingly been a part of. None of the other federal agencies had been concerned about that.

And Lia hadn't had anywhere to go anyway.

So Agent Wood had connected her with Zach Simmons, and Lia's future had been changed from a giant question mark of *nothing*, to a life. And her life in Hope Town was *everything*. She didn't want to mess it up.

But she hadn't realized it was still only half a life until Sammy had swept into the bakery and stolen from her. Gard and Sammy were becoming everything too, and she didn't know how to *choose*.

"Furthermore," Zach continued. "What happened to Albennie happened because her situation is a little more… dangerous. And tenuous. You don't have to compare yourself to her. You're not an active target. She was."

"I just want everyone to be safe."

Zach nodded. "I built Hope Town for…hope. Or I would have called it Survival Town, Lia. You get to be a person and have a life. That comes with making choices about how you share your past and to who. This isn't traditional WitSec. It was never supposed to be. The goal is to keep the people who come here safe. I don't see how…someone knowing your involvement in bringing down a trafficking ring seven years ago, particularly when that someone is a cop…is putting anyone at risk. It goes without saying you can't share anyone else's story, or explain how many of you are here, but your story is your own. If you're looking for permission or approval to share it, you have it."

Lia sat there staring at Zach. The words didn't quite… make sense. Or they did, but she couldn't quite absorb them.

"Did you really come here for permission?" Zach asked

gently. "Or were you hoping I'd tell you that you have to keep your secrets?"

She blinked at Zach. He was a friend, kind of. But, at the end of the day, he knew more about her life than anyone. He knew every part of what had brought her here.

And he wasn't exactly wrong to ask that question. He wasn't exactly right either. It wasn't that she *wanted* to keep her secrets. It was just that she'd held on to them so long, she didn't really know *how* to let them go.

"I just…have to tell him. That's what I know."

"I appreciate you coming to me. This conversation. It's a reminder that I need to be a little…flexible. Lives and situations change, especially the deeper we get into this, the longer some of you are here. There aren't going to be one-size-fits-all rules for anyone who lives here. You might have all come here to be safe, but everyone's situation is different and needs a different touch."

Lia thought about Albennie being an active target. Which meant other people probably were too. But no one else here was involved in *her* past. *Her* story.

"Your life in Hope Town doesn't change, Lia, if you open it up beyond that. That's not what we're about."

Open it up beyond Hope Town. When she hadn't even realized she'd shrunk it down *to* Hope Town. But she had, and that wasn't on Hope Town or Zach or rules. It was on her.

And she didn't want that anymore. She wanted more. She got to her feet and managed to smile at Zach. "I just hope you know, if this place didn't exist, I would have been lost a long time ago."

He smiled back. "Well, I guess it's a good thing it exists, then."

Chapter Thirteen

Lia hurried back to her house, a little later than she'd planned. Gard was supposed to get here at five. A little early for dinner, but since Sammy would be dropped off back at his place around nine, they wanted time.

Alone time.

It was already four thirty and she still had to shower the bakery day off of her. Luckily, the roast and potatoes were already in the oven, and the green beans were in the Crock-Pot, but she still needed to bake the rolls—though they were all proofed and shaped and ready to go.

She threw them in the oven after the shower, then rushed back to her bathroom to dry her hair.

Gard liked it down. Which gave her a little thrill, admittedly. She *liked* the way his eyes darkened when she left it down. The way she'd find him staring at her intently. Of course, he did that sometimes when her hair was up. When they were at the bakery surrounded by people or in the dark making out in front of her car before she drove home from his house.

But there were no teenagers waiting for them tonight. At least, not until nine.

And who knew when that was likely to happen again, so she had to seize the day, the moment.

After she told him about her past.

And if that's kind of a big, fat turnoff, Lia?

She didn't have time to consider that because someone knocked on her door. Nerves jangling, she opened it to Gard standing on her porch.

Her heart just *tripped* over itself every time she saw him. She'd never had that feeling before. Maybe too mired in survival mode to notice anyone else, but more likely just… *him*. There couldn't be too many guys like Gard.

He was dressed casually, and he'd gotten a haircut sometime since Wednesday when she'd seen him last. His blue eyes traveled over her quickly, and his mouth curved. "Hi."

"Hi. Um, come in." She moved out of the way, gestured him inside. He somehow looked taller in here—like all her stuff had been made for smaller people, when she wasn't exactly *short*.

"Something smells amazing."

"I hope it tastes as good as it smells. I don't cook a lot since it's just me and I bake all day. The rolls, I can guarantee you, will be excellent." She didn't feel nervous very often around Gard anymore but knowing that there was this…other step they were dancing toward had her stomach absolutely jumping.

"It's a nice place," he said, following her deeper into the house. The kitchen was separated from the dining room by a long counter. She didn't ever eat in her dining room, using it usually as more space to put things she was baking or experimenting with, but she'd set the table tonight so her and Gard could.

"I just have a few last touches for dinner." She pulled the rolls out of the oven. "Did you get a lunch today?"

Sometimes he worked through lunch, usually when he forgot to make himself one in the morning because he was rushing around trying to get Sammy to school. She liked that she knew little details like that. It made her feel like a part of their lives even when she wasn't there.

"Uh, no, I guess I didn't," he said. Distracted.

She looked at him over her shoulder. He was staring out the window in her dining room. He had that pensive look on his face he usually only got when he was worried about Sammy. Which she supposed made sense. The girls were at a movie without parental supervision tonight, even if the parents were giving rides.

She turned off the oven and crossed to him.

"Everything okay?" she asked, putting her hand on his back.

He turned into the touch, and she reached up to brush a hand over his hair. She liked the thickness of it, the different shades of blond. She liked feeling like she had a right to ask him if things were okay and touch him with reassurance that they would be.

He settled his hands on her waist. "Yeah, just…work stuff."

"Can you not tell me about work stuff?" She'd understand if he couldn't. Probably better than he could fathom.

"I can, I just… I don't really want to think about it right now." He pulled her closer, and his mouth curved. She could tell he was trying very hard to smile, so she leaned into him. The tall, strong *wall* of him and that intent way he had of looking at her. Flutters turned into full-on *pangs*.

The strong, sensual pull of desire mixed with something achy in her chest like wanting to fix everything in the world for him.

So she pushed onto her toes and pressed her mouth to his. Just a gentle, reassuring kiss before they sat down and ate, and talked. Because they really did need to talk. After she told him everything, he'd understand and…

But Gard's hands tightened on her hips, and the soft, reassuring kiss turned into something…sharper. Needier. Which swept through her in an instant. That pull. This *want* they'd had to put on the back burner for Sammy.

A worthy cause, but not a necessary one in this moment.

"Can dinner keep?" he murmured against her mouth.

She nodded, wrapping her arms around his neck. Anything could keep.

Except this.

He lifted her off her feet, and she laughed breathlessly against his mouth at how easily he'd just hooked his arms under her butt and carried her deeper into her house. It was a little thrill, how strong he was. How *easy* it was for him to unerringly find her bedroom. Carefully lay her down on her bed and then cover her entire body with his.

She sighed into the sturdy weight of him. Being horizontal was *quite* the improvement to all their very vertical kissing. Everything about this was an improvement.

The way he touched her. The way she could touch him—pulling off his shirt, smoothing her hands over the impressive muscles of his arms, his chest. His hands on her bare skin, unclasping her bra. Losing pieces of clothing one by one until they moved together in one quiet rush and stilled…like they *both* felt that reverberating gong of *right*. This, right here. Just…right.

Gard looked down at her, eyes blue and intense and… everything. He was so handsome. So good. She didn't know how she'd stumbled into finding *this*, but it was everything.

His mouth touched hers again, gentle, drugging, meaningful. Then just like in the other room, it sharpened. Need. Urgency. *Now.*

Then the heady race over edge after edge, until Gard fell with her and they tangled up together on her bed. Gard held her close as they both struggled to catch their breath.

She realized, very belatedly, she hadn't had a chance to tell him all the things she was supposed to.

Oh well. She snuggled closer into him, reveling in this closeness, this intimacy, in *him*.

She still would tell him everything. Over dinner. He'd tell her about work, and she'd tell him about her past and…

And if the moment felt right, maybe she'd even admit that her feelings for him were…probably a little deeper than he was ready for. Maybe.

She thought about the way he'd looked down at her. That intensity, but something more. That warmth, but something a little hesitant. Like he felt it too.

Maybe he did. He was holding her tight. He'd folded her into his life, but more than that, he'd let Sammy fold her into Sammy's life. That *meant* something to a man like Gard.

Maybe…

The future was full of maybes, and for the first time in a long time, that felt like a gift instead of a curse.

Gard lay in Lia's bed, holding her close. The pillow smelled like whatever her hair smelled like. Some kind of fruity shampoo he'd like to inhale forever.

Forever.

He'd never felt like this, and he knew what that meant. He had enough friends who were married to know that the path to *that* started with a woman who felt different than the ones who'd come before.

Lia just slotted into place, and even though it left him a little uneasy over how he was going to make that work—his profession wasn't exactly an easy one to build a partnership around. Add being the guardian to a surly teenager with some major baggage and there were likely to be all kinds of hurdles and pressures and struggles.

But he knew people who did it, who made relationships work and raised kids right along with it. He could make it work, even with a little bit of unease, because…

A life with Lia in it looked…a hell of a lot better than it had without.

Which meant he couldn't chicken out of telling her that he was in love with her. And he wasn't going to. He'd just had a bad day at work dealing with a particularly ugly domestic assault and thought maybe he'd wait until he felt a little less like there was no hope for humanity.

Then he'd walked into her house that had smelled amazing, and she'd looked so pretty and happy to see him, and she'd asked him what was wrong and he'd just…

He'd figured the talking part could come later. And it would. Because of course it was the right moment to tell her. She was always the right moment.

She slid away from him. "I better go make sure I didn't leave any burners on. Don't want to start any fires out of distraction."

He let her get out of the bed, watched in appreciation for a moment or two while she pulled on her clothes before he followed suit. Yes, a good love declaration should probably include clothes. More serious, less heat of the moment. So she understood how…important it was. How weighty.

He'd managed to get his pants on, but before he'd pulled his shirt on, his phone chimed—the sound he had assigned only to Sammy's contact number. He swore under his breath. When it chimed again, he realized it was an incoming call, not just a text. He couldn't imagine why she'd call him while hanging out with her friends unless it was something bad.

He fumbled for the phone. "Sammy, what's up?" he answered, trying to sound calm. "Everything okay?"

"Uh… Mr. Fairhurst. This is Sarabeth."

His entire stomach plummeted.

"What's wrong?"

"I don't know." And the normally confident, straightforward girl sounded *scared*. "We can't find Sammy."

For a quick, blinding moment there was nothing but abject terror. Then he felt Lia's warm hand on his shoulder.

He pulled himself together. "What do you mean you can't find her? Is the movie over?"

"No. She… She said she had to go to the bathroom. She left her purse with Izzy, and her phone was in it. But she never came back. It's been like thirty minutes now. We went looking for her, and we can't find her. She's not in the bathroom. She's not anywhere. I called Henry. He's coming. He told me to call you."

"I'm on my way. Just stay put, all right? Even when Henry gets there. Stay put until I get there, okay?"

"I don't know where she would have gone. Not without her phone. Not by herself."

"We'll find out. Just sit tight. It'll be all right." He hung up the phone, shoved it in his pocket and then raked his fingers through his hair. "I have to go."

"What is it, Gard? The girls can't find Sammy? What does that mean?"

He told her exactly what Sarabeth had said while he pulled on his shirt then got his shoes back on. He headed for the door, brain swirling with worries and fears and too many terrible work stories to fight back. His only clear thought was he had to get to that movie theater.

When he opened her front door, he realized Lia was shoving her feet into shoes too and grabbing her purse.

"Lia—"

"I'm coming with," she said, her tone brooking no room for argument.

But he wanted to argue with her. Even opened his mouth to. This was *his* responsibility, and he was failing Dani and Sammy *again*, and he didn't need a spectator to pick up the pieces he'd broken.

Not your fault, he reminded himself, because self-flagellation didn't save his sister or his niece. And neither did pushing Lia away, because he could see the worry in her expression and she… She loved Sammy too. This wasn't just on *him* anymore.

And, more, she had more insight into Sammy, the teenager with a rough life. Maybe Lia would see something he didn't. Sammy was always telling him his *cop brain* got in the way of being a real human.

"Make sure those burners are off," he told her gruffly.

She nodded and hurried to the kitchen, then returned, keys hanging out of her hands. They walked outside, Lia locking her front door in quick efficient movements.

They got into his truck without saying anything, but once he'd backed out of her drive, Lia took his hand. She held his hand in a tight squeeze the entire drive to Fairmont.

He didn't let himself think this was some kind of punishment for enjoying himself.

He'd save that for later.

Besides, it was just a mistake. A mix-up. He'd get there and Sammy would be…fine.

He told himself that the whole drive there.

Chapter Fourteen

Lia had to jog to keep up with Gard as he strode toward the movie theater. He was doing an impressive job of appearing fine and in control. It was the *cop* in him clearly that knew how to shut off the fear. Even when he'd called someone at the police department, he'd sounded like he was in complete control.

But she also knew him well enough to know where to look. The tight jaw, the desolate look in his eyes, that was all worry and fear. Outside he might seem calm and in control, but inside he was a mess.

Then again, so was she. There was no reason she could think of that would make Sammy pull this kind of stunt. Particularly not without her phone. Lia couldn't find a spin on the situation that didn't involve Sammy being in danger.

So she held on to Gard's outward calm as an example of how to be, even while her insides panicked.

Inside in the lobby of the movie theater, Sarabeth stood with her parents, and Izzy with hers. Everyone turned to Gard as he approached.

"Still no sign of her?" he demanded.

Everyone shook their heads.

"She was fine," Izzy said quietly. "Nothing was out of the ordinary. She just didn't come back." There were tears in the girl's eyes, and she leaned into her dad when he put his arm around her shoulders.

"I talked to the theater manager," a tall man standing next to Sarabeth said in low tones. Presumably Sarabeth's stepfather. "He was going to go see what kind of security footage they had."

"Good," Gard said in that firm, cop voice. "Do you know where he went?"

"I'll show you."

The two men walked off.

"She wouldn't have left her purse if she meant to run away," Izzy said, her voice an octave higher than usual. "She wouldn't have. She specifically gave it to me to hold." Izzy looked up at her dad like she was looking for reassurance.

"And nothing…happened?" Lia asked. "She didn't mention anything upsetting her?" It was hard to believe Sammy would scare *everyone*, especially her friends, by just up and disappearing. But if she was upset about something, maybe she hadn't been thinking clearly. Maybe she'd just… taken a walk.

Still, leaving that damn phone behind? Why would she do that? *She wouldn't.*

"No. She was in a good mood," Sarabeth said. "I swear, everything was *normal*. She would have told us if it wasn't. Not just…ditched us. With her purse."

"Do you still have her purse?"

Izzy held it out and Lia looked through it. Wallet. Chap-Stick. Phone. Lia pulled the phone out and tapped the screen. The background was a picture of Sarabeth, Izzy, and Sammy—probably taken at the sleepover.

Lia wanted to cry at how sweet and happy they all looked, but she blinked back tears. Lia didn't know her passcode, but no doubt Gard did. She started to walk in the direction he'd gone with Sarabeth's stepdad, but they were already returning.

Gard held up a hand in a greeting and Lia looked behind her. A woman and a man were striding toward them. They didn't wear uniforms, but Lia had a feeling they were cops just the same.

"Thomas." Sarabeth threw her arms around the man, who gave her a reassuring pat on the back.

The woman approached Gard while this Thomas talked to the girls.

"I figured it would be quicker if we just came straight out rather than the extra step of a deputy. Hart's got connections to the Thompsons and the Hudsons," she said, gesturing at the man talking to the girls. "So he wanted to come in case anything needed smoothing over on that front."

"Thanks, Laurel. I've got a kid trying to pull together the security footage to show us, but he doesn't know what he's doing. He put in a call to the day manager for help."

"Good start," Laurel said with a nod.

Lia didn't want to interrupt, but she was still holding Sammy's phone. She held it out. "Gard. Maybe you should look through her phone."

He nodded, taking the phone and typing in the code without a second thought. He swore almost immediately and tipped the screen so Lia could see too. It was a text conversation between Sammy and…*Mom*. Dani.

While Gard explained the conversation to the detective, Lia read through the exchange.

I know you're mad at me, but I want to see you.

No.

Pls, Sammy. PLEASE.

I'm @ movies w my friends. Leave me alone.

Meet me outside the theater. Out back. Just give me 5 mins. Pls.

Fine.

Lia's heart seized. Oh…no. But she tried to smooth it over for Gard. "Well, she's with Dani. That's…not terrible. It could be worse. Maybe you could call Dani."

Gard didn't even look at her. He kept talking to the woman. A detective, Lia thought, if she was reading all the context clues.

"I called for help, Laurel, but I'm going to be looking for my niece," Gard said, an edge of temper starting to creep into his voice. "You're working with Beckett on that trafficking case coming out of Hardy, right?"

At the word *trafficking*, everything jangling around inside of Lia like fear and worry and nerves turned into cold, sharp *ice*.

"Trafficking?" she echoed.

But Gard was still ignoring her, or maybe he didn't even hear her. Deep in cop mode, he was ignoring everything except what he needed to do. "Dani was with that guy in that security footage of the drug deal. I want to know everything about him, what connections he has. If Dani was with him, he has to know something about where she's been and where she might have taken Sammy."

Lia thought back to everything Gard had told her about Dani's disappearance. The job offer at the diner. The abandoned house with drug paraphernalia. But he hadn't mentioned *trafficking*, and it made too many things click into place.

Particularly that text conversation that Lia couldn't be convinced was actually from Dani now. Which made her blood run cold.

"Gard." She curled her fingers into his shirtsleeve. "I need to talk to you."

He didn't respond. She didn't think he was ignoring her on purpose. He was just deep in crisis, and she was just…a civilian in his way. He was used to shutting everything out that didn't accomplish getting the job done.

Except she…she knew things, understood things. About everything they were talking about. And everything was starting to coalesce. The things he'd told her he'd found out about Dani the past few months.

The things she'd experienced years ago.

"Gard. Please." She tugged on his shirt. "Somewhere private." Maybe it was the *please*, or the fact her voice cracked, but he finally looked at her, blinked like coming out of a trance.

"Okay." He took her hand and squeezed. "Get her description out," he told Laurel.

Who nodded. "I will. Then Hart and I will interview theater employees after he's done getting the girls' statements. We'll watch that footage too, once it's ready. Get a read on anyone who might have been involved."

Gard nodded and then let Lia pull him away from the hubbub into a quiet little alcove.

She should have told him the truth earlier, when they had time. But now there was no time.

Not if she was going to help Sammy.

GARD WASN'T PANICKING. He'd been a cop too long to panic.

Or so he told himself.

"I need you to listen to me and not worry about questions

right now," Lia said quietly, and very, *very* seriously. "We can answer questions later. Right now, we need to focus. This job offer Dani got. You know who offered it, right?"

He frowned at her. She sounded like…a cop. And he didn't have the first clue why she'd be talking about Dani's job offer. Still, he answered her since she clearly had some reason for pulling him aside. "I have a name, yeah."

"You need to—or *they* need to—go get that guy too. He's your target as much as whoever was with her in that drug deal. The guy who offered the job at the diner will know something. I guarantee it."

He didn't want to be curt, because he knew Lia meant well, but he didn't have time for this. "Lia, no offense but—"

"I know a thing or two about human trafficking, Gard. I know what it looks like. *That's* what it looks like. Job offers to the right targets. Addresses that are seemingly abandoned or vacant. Then pulling more people in."

He blinked. She had a serious expression on her face and those words were hard. Knowledgeable. Cop-like.

I know a thing or two about human trafficking. Not like she'd read a book or seen a movie, like she *knew*.

"And the fact of the matter is," she continued. "Those text messages might have come from Dani's phone, but that doesn't mean they necessarily came from Dani."

He could only stare at her, those words not quite making sense in the way he knew they should. But this was… Lia. And… "Lia, what are you saying?"

"I'm saying that this has all the hallmarks of a kidnapping. And if you're working on a trafficking case, and Dani is connected, Sammy would be an obvious and easy target to be pulled into that."

He was trying very hard not to think of all the *worsts*, but Lia's calm, factual determinations made it impossible.

She reached out and grabbed his arms. "I need you to tell me everything about that case."

His brain felt scrambled, because he needed to know how *she* knew all this stuff, but he didn't have time. If *anything* she was saying was true, he had to find Sammy. Now.

So he told her what he knew. She stood there and listened. He'd never seen this expression on her face. So serious, so grim.

Laurel approached them, but he'd managed to tell Lia just about everything at that point.

"We've got Sammy on video going out the back of the theater, which points to her meeting your sister out there like the text message said. But no one was caught on video in the back in the right time frame, so if it was Dani, she stayed out of sight. We're going to canvas the parking lot, see if we can find anyone who saw something."

Gard nodded. He glanced at Lia and that serious expression he'd never seen. "I want us looking for Roger Hamilton—the guy who used the Dry Road address. On top of anyone in that security video of the drug deal."

"We can poke into those different angles, Fairhurst. I get that you're worried, and I'm going to do everything to help, but keep in mind it's kind of a leap. Just because Dani was in that drug deal video doesn't mean Sammy's disappearance connects beyond Dani wanting to talk to her daughter. They could have gone somewhere to talk privately. I'm willing to investigate, but this might not be worst case scenario."

"I'd love that to be the case, but I can't hope for better and not prepare for worse. Not with Sammy at risk. You need to look into Roger Hamilton."

"I really don't see how the job offer Dani got—"

"It connects," Lia said firmly, earning her a very suspicious glare from Laurel.

"That house you went to when you broke your nose, Gard. Dani had that address. I know you didn't find anything, but there's something to that," Lia said, clearly not fazed by Laurel's hard look. "And it connecting to the guy who offered her this shady job means there's something to that too."

"There wasn't any evidence of anything going on in that house except drugs," Laurel said, still eyeing Lia suspiciously. "Maybe Roger Hamilton wasn't in the drug deal security footage, but that doesn't mean this isn't just…drugs."

"Gard, Dani has disappeared a lot on you before because of drugs. Does this follow any pattern of those times?" Lia demanded.

He couldn't *count* the ways this had been abnormal, and he'd just kept having to shove that knowledge away, convinced he was grasping for straws. And now…it was possible he wasn't.

He felt sick to his stomach. "No."

"No, because it's not *just* drugs. It's something more. Something bigger. That house with the drugs is likely a… staging area, you'd call it. A centralized party location. So yes, drugs. But they're doing the deals in Hardy, and they're keeping Dani *somewhere* out of sight. If there are other missing women… No one would be *kept* at the party house. But they'd be nearby. What about some kind of outbuilding on the property? Or a cellar? Not in sight of the house, but close."

Gard looked over at Laurel, who was staring at Lia with that same suspicion. But she didn't voice it.

"I'd have to double-check with Beckett, but I don't think

they got a warrant to search the property beyond the house," Laurel said.

Gard exchanged a look with Lia. He wasn't waiting for any damn warrant, and clearly she didn't think he should either.

"I'll work on a search warrant for the surrounding property," Laurel said, like she could read his mind. "Look, I know you have to find her, and you're not on duty so whatever you're about to do is your business. I'm not telling you not to. All I'm saying is we also want to put these guys behind bars, so while me and the other Bent County officers on duty are following the letter of the law…try not to get in the way of that."

Gard didn't say anything.

"I'll put Beckett on finding Roger Hamilton. Hart will hold down the fort here, see if we can track down someone who saw something. I'll coordinate warrants and whatever else we need. Leave your cell on in case we find her," Laurel said, then she strode away.

Gard took Lia by the arm, began ushering her out of the theater. "Can Albennie come pick you up? Or Franny? Hell, I can call Royal and—"

"I'm coming with you, Gard."

"You can't come with, Lia."

"I have to," she replied stubbornly. "I know what you need to look for and look out for. I'm the best chance you've got."

Yeah, he really wanted to know *how*, but he didn't have time. "This is police business."

"You're not going as a cop. You're going as an uncle. And a brother. Which means it's not police business for you. Which means I'm going *with* you."

"I'm going with a *gun*."

She stopped and looked up at him. Still grim, but now with some determination in that grimness too. It was almost a relief.

Determination felt like an active positive. Grim had felt…like the worst had already happened.

"You can leave me here, but I'll only follow. You can't cut me out of this. It's too important, and I offer too much."

He didn't know what to do with this. Lia wasn't someone who lied or exaggerated. She never acted like she thought she was any tougher than she was, but how could he just let her come *with*? This could be dangerous. He had training. He knew how to deal with criminals.

But the way she was talking…maybe she did too.

Still. The thought of her in the middle of all this…

He reached out, cupped her face with his hands. "How am I supposed to save them if I have to worry about you?" And he had to save them. God, he'd let this go on so long, convinced it was…

He couldn't think about that now.

"I can find them, Gard," she said, so seriously, reaching up and putting her hands over his. "And I can handle myself. I always have."

He didn't want to risk it, but…if Lia was right, if she really understood what was going on here better than he did, Dani and Sammy were in so much more danger than he wanted to believe.

And he needed Lia to make sure he saved them.

"Let's go then."

Chapter Fifteen

Lia hopped into Gard's truck. Determination had replaced some of her panic. She had the experience, the knowledge, the understanding to save Sammy before anything terrible happened. She knew what to look for. She could *help*.

She'd saved people before. She'd put these kinds of men behind bars before. Sure, with the help of the FBI, but today she had the help of a cop. And some detectives, even if the female one had clearly been suspicious of her.

They were all willing to help, to try. They weren't like the cops who'd harassed her when she'd been a runaway teen. They wanted to *help*.

And Gard was letting her help, even without knowing why. So it was all going to be okay, because she and Gard would do *anything* to bring Sammy home safe.

So fear wasn't the predominant feeling. Just a vague background one underneath her absolute determination to do whatever she could, however she could.

"While we drive, explain to me how you know this stuff," Gard said as he pulled out onto the highway. His words were clipped. Not angry, exactly, but the sharp edge to his tone still had her stiffening.

Lia blew out an unsteady breath. He deserved this explanation, and it would help him trust she knew what she was doing. But it…hurt. That this was how she had to tell him about it.

Hurt couldn't matter with Sammy at stake though.

So Lia tried to organize her thoughts. She needed to tell the story as concisely as possible. They could hash out details later. Once Sammy was safe. There was only so much time for understanding as Gard sped down the dark highway out toward this place on Dry Road.

"When my friend and I ran away, it was because this guy had offered her a job, like I told you. She told me they were happy for her to bring in more people—if I made a good impression. So, this guy picks us up and takes us to this…party, and my friend says if I impress the bosses, they'll let me stay."

She couldn't think about how vulnerable and desperate she'd been to believe this story. To *go* and then try to impress a group of grown *men* that she was somehow worthy of their "job." She couldn't think of Dani and Sammy being in the same situation.

She had to focus on the proving to Gard that she belonged here, trying to help them.

"Everything seemed… I mean, it was a little scary because they were mostly adults, and I was definitely the youngest person there, but no one did anything…scary. There were drugs and alcohol. My friend took something, but I stayed clear of that. My parents' death weighed too heavily on me for that. But I figured drinking was okay."

Getting off track. Too many details. "Anyway, at the time, I was naive. I didn't know what it was about, and I didn't really know enough to know how scared I should be. Everyone seemed to be having fun. Then there was this guy… He was the second in command. Important. I remembered my friend saying I was supposed to impress him in particular."

Lia struggled to swallow past the way her throat tightened. She didn't like to remember. But she had to.

"In the moment, it felt like he was really nice to me. As time went on, he was…protective. He wouldn't let me take on any of these mysterious jobs like my friend did. He just…kept me with him. For the first time in my life, it felt like someone cared. I know *now* he didn't, but at the time I was a desperate, messed-up teenager. And he made me feel important. While my friend went to work, so-called, he kept me with him and told me I was his princess, and my life should be easy."

She felt vaguely ill, but she had to push through. "I guess I knew something wasn't right, but if I asked questions, he'd get mad at me, so I stopped asking questions. I just… enjoyed being his…" The words stuck in her throat, but she had to force them out. "I guess I thought I was his girlfriend. In the moment. And while my friend…disappeared, never to be seen again, and I saw questionable things happen around me, nothing bad ever happened to *me*."

"He never…" Gard trailed off, clearly struggling to find the right words. But Lia knew what he was asking.

"He didn't have to…force me to do anything. I thought it was… I thought he…" She didn't have time to be squeamish, ashamed, embarrassed. "I thought he cared about me. And I didn't realize he was manipulating me. Not then."

She'd dealt with this in therapy. The strange dichotomy of never having said *no*, but being a victim all the same.

"So, I was considered his and protected by him for a few years. Towards the end…he started to get a little violent, but it was better than what happened to the other girls. By

that time, I was starting to understand they were getting…
sold off, mistreated. A few slaps was hardly as bad as that."

She couldn't look at Gard when she said that. She
couldn't think about him at all. She just had to get through
the story.

"At some point, we were at this concert—a whole group
of us. And I kind of got separated and this woman approached me. She was very direct. She told me she was an
FBI agent, and that she could help me get out of this trafficking ring. I told her I didn't need help, and there was no
trafficking and she was crazy. But I took her contact information, and I hid it from JJ."

Lia could still physically feel how terrified she'd been.
Terrified the woman was right. Terrified JJ would find out
and this tenuous grasp she had on survival would be over.

"But I didn't tell him about her. I wasn't going to help
her, because I didn't want to stir things up. Except then…
These new girls came in. And I could see… Something was
changing. JJ didn't want me anymore. He wanted this…
younger girl. Younger than even I'd been when I first got
there, and that's when I started to…question things. I knew
what happened once you were discarded. It wasn't pretty.
And I knew… In ways I couldn't see when I was the young
one he was using, how messed up it was. He was a grown
man, and this girl was *thirteen*. So, I started to plan. Not
because I wanted to do any good—just because I didn't
want the bad things to happen to me."

"It clearly wasn't just for yourself, Lia," Gard said, his
voice oddly…tight. "Or you wouldn't have cared that the
other girl was thirteen."

Lia didn't know about that. She'd absolved herself of a
lot of things she'd done without knowing better, but that
still felt like…the kind of thing a bad person did. A self-

ish, horrible person. Because at that point she *had* started to know better.

So she ignored his comment. "I contacted the FBI agent, and I worked with her. She told me what to look for, what to ask about. She told me the signs and I gave her all the information she needed to bring them down. Three years too late, but I brought them down."

"It wasn't too late for the people you helped save, Lia. At what? Eighteen? You don't get to play that down. Not to me."

Still, she couldn't…engage with that. With the way her chest felt too tight and tears pricked in her eyes. Because this wasn't about *her*. It was about Sammy.

"But it all adds up. The job offer. The drug house. The suspected trafficking ring. They won't have multiple properties. They're too small-time in a town as small as Hardy— probably some offshoot of something bigger. Maybe even just a stopping point in a ring. If they have that abandoned house as their party center, the people they're keeping— against their will or not—will be nearby."

She noted Gard was slowing down the truck's pace. The road was dark—not a light to be seen anywhere except his headlights. They had to be getting close.

He pulled to a stop on the side of the road, turned the truck's lights off. "It'll probably be best to approach on foot." He paused. "I don't suppose there's any chance you'll stay here?"

"Not one."

He sighed heavily. "All right. Here's what we're going to do. We're going to walk down the road until we get to the address. Our only goal right now is to find Sammy. Everything else comes second to that."

He reached across to the glove compartment, stuck his

key in, and opened it. He pulled out a gun. Lia knew she shouldn't feel uncomfortable. God knew they might need it, and Gard knew what he was doing. She might have some insight into trafficking groups, but he was a *cop.*

"You're going to do what I say, Lia. And you're going to stay behind me. I'm trusting your knowledge of this kind of situation, but you have to trust my cop instincts. We can't save Sammy if we're not safe, so you have to listen. Do you understand?"

"Yes," she said, nodding emphatically. She didn't want to cause problems or ruin anything. She just wanted to help.

You've done this before. You'll do it again.

"All right, let's go."

They got out of the truck. The night was frigid and dark and Lia had to blink back tears of fear. Gard skirted the truck and grabbed her hand, warm and steady.

"Lia, I'm sorry all that happened to you," he said, very quietly, very sincerely.

Her throat tightened. It meant something, not just that he'd say it, but make sure to say it now so she understood, just like she'd always kind of expected, Gard wasn't going to hold her past against her. That he'd seen enough to learn grace, and he was strong enough, good enough to lean into that over resentment.

"I am too. I'm sorry about a lot of things that happened to me." She squeezed his hand. "But, Gard, if it helps us find Sammy and bring her home, I don't care. It'll be worth it."

GARD REALLY DIDN'T want Lia by his side right now. This was too dangerous. Worrying about her split his focus.

But he couldn't deny her story meant she understood the ins and outs of something he'd never dealt with. Sure, he'd had some training here and there about what to look for when it came to trafficking, but nothing this in-depth.

Certainly not an actual inside view.

He'd heard the guilt, the self-blame in Lia's voice, but all he could think was she'd been *fifteen*. She'd survived that abuse for three years and then worked with an *FBI agent* to bring down an entire trafficking ring. How could she look back at that with anything but pride?

Once they found Sammy—*and* Dani—and got them home and safe, he'd deal with that. For right now, he had to put everything Lia had said and been through out of his mind and focus. He had to be a cop.

But a cop wouldn't be holding a civilian's hand as they walked down a dark, deserted road in the middle of nowhere. A cop would know better.

He didn't have time to think or worry about that, because Sammy had been taken somewhere. He didn't want to believe Dani had done that to her. If he let himself consider that, he'd be absolutely destroyed, and he couldn't afford that.

So he chose to believe, like Lia had said, it hadn't actually been Dani texting Sammy. Of course, that didn't put Sammy in any better of a situation or ease his fear for her safety any.

They walked and walked, and Gard knew it was taking too long, but he couldn't run in the dark. Even with his eyes adjusted to the darkness, it took all his concentration to follow the side of the road and count the gravel drives until they finally made it to the one they needed.

Before they even made it a few steps, he heard sounds. Quite a ways before the light from the house came into view. The faint beat of music, a lilt of too-loud laughter, the murmur of voices. He hurried his pace, pulling Lia along until he could see the house.

Lights shone from every cracked or broken window. Shadows moved inside. Shafts of light spilled out onto the overgrown yard, but it was clear no one was paying attention to what was going on outside. They were having some kind of party in there.

Gard started to walk forward, moved the safety on his gun off, but Lia tugged at his hand.

"Gard," she said on a firm whisper. "You can't go in there on your own. They'll have guns, and a lot of them will be high. It's a party right now."

"And if Sammy and Dani are in there?" he whispered back.

"Maybe they are. Maybe they aren't. But there's absolutely no way for you to go in guns blazing and have it turn out well for *anyone*. Look." She pointed at the house. "There are at least ten people in there. And that's just what we can see from this front window, so probably more. I guarantee you they have weapons of their own, and they're high so they're going to do something foolish. Don't do something foolish right along with them."

She wasn't wrong. He watched the windows. But what if Dani and Sammy were one of the people walking around in there? Didn't that mean he needed to *act*?

Not if you walk in there and get you and Lia killed.

"Let's see if we can find a barn or shed or something," Lia was saying. "If we can find where they're keeping people… And Laurel gets that search warrant, it's all over. If Dani and Sammy are in there, it's just partying right now. They'll be okay, and if you can get a reason for enough of a police presence, they'll be able to raid the party without anyone getting hurt."

He wondered if she believed that or if she was just that good of an actress. But she wasn't *wrong*. Even if Dani and Sammy were in there and *not* okay, he couldn't rush in without some kind of backup. It wouldn't save anyone. It'd just hurt them all.

And *legal backup* couldn't come without the warrants Laurel was trying to get.

He turned away from the house, dropping Lia's hand and pulling his phone out of his pocket. He doubted anyone inside would be looking out down the drive, but if they did his body should block the light of his phone.

"I'm going to text Royal. He's off duty. It's a risk for him to help me with this when—"

Lia put her hand on his shoulder. "I'm sure he'll be more than willing to help. Royal isn't afraid of some risks."

Royal was still just one guy, but maybe he could bring along that brother-in-law of his who Gard was pretty sure had some kind of military background. And Royal had an interesting background himself, not that Gard knew the details.

Did everyone connected to Hope Town have secret pasts? He didn't have time to consider that.

But more bodies meant more chance of this situation not escalating. So Gard sent a quick, concise text to his friend, including the address and instructions to wait at the drive.

Because even if Royal could jump to help immediately, this place was a ways away from Hope Town and Sunrise and Bent. It would take Royal and whoever else time to get here, and Gard couldn't wait for that.

It didn't take more than a minute for the response to come through.

Should be there in about twenty. Zeke might be able to round up a few more. More soon.

Gard let out an unsteady breath. Royal hadn't asked one question, hadn't hesitated. Now Gard just had to hope he could find a way to get Dani and Sammy out of this without jeopardizing the police work necessary to stop this group.

Because he was going to do whatever it took to get Dani and Sammy safe—even if it meant ruining a police investigation and losing his badge.

"He's coming. Maybe more than just him."

"Good, that's a start," Lia said. "Let's see if we can find an outbuilding while we wait."

He took Lia's hand again in silent agreement, but this time, he let her lead. Apparently she knew what she was looking for.

In the dark, everything was a shadow, and the lights from the house only illuminated so far. So he wasn't sure they'd be able to see something even if there *was* another building. But what if Sammy or Dani or both were in this place Lia was so sure existed? Surely if they were captives, they wouldn't be inside that party.

He wasn't sure how long they walked, and he didn't ask Lia if she could see, if she really knew where she was leading them. If he started questioning her now, the whole thing fell apart and no matter what doubts and concerns he had, he knew one thing.

Lia wouldn't jeopardize Sammy for anything. So whatever she thought she was doing, it was the right thing. Even if Gard didn't fully understand.

So he followed, straining his eyes in the dark. Even the lights on in the house couldn't illuminate things way back here. The grass was overgrown but mostly dying off thanks to the encroaching winter. His nose, hands, and feet were cold, but he didn't really register just how frigid it was.

He just kept walking, searching the night for some sign

of *something*. Because Lia thought something else should be here. If they could find Sammy and Dani out here, maybe they could secret them out without any kind of showdown.

He wasn't sure how long they'd walked when Lia must have tripped over something, because she lost her footing on an *oof*. He managed to keep her upright since they were holding hands, but they both looked down to whatever she'd tripped over.

The shadow on the ground seemed like some kind of lump.

"It was kind of…soft," Lia muttered. Then a little light popped on—the light from Lia's phone, just barely illuminating the heap in front of them.

It was a body.

Lifeless. Blond hair matted with dirt and what was probably blood.

Gard didn't need to be able to see the face to know who it was.

"Dani."

Chapter Sixteen

Lia crouched down on the side of the motionless woman at the same time Gard did.

"She's breathing," Lia said, since she could hear the labored rise and fall of the woman's breath. "Gard, she's breathing." But she wasn't sure he heard her. Or anything.

Dani clearly wasn't conscious, and Gard was clearly dealing with his own version of panic, hidden under a stillness that worried Lia.

In the dim beam of Lia's phone's flashlight, she saw Gard's hands shake as he gently took the woman's shoulder and rolled her over on to her back. She lolled lifelessly, but Gard put a hand to her neck, checking her pulse.

Lia couldn't take her gaze away from the deep gash across her forehead though. It was oozing blood. She was *not* in good shape. Lia couldn't tell for sure from the dim light, but it looked like there were bruises on her face and neck too.

"Breathing. A pulse," Gard said, his whisper as shaky as his hands. "Come on, Dani. Wake up for me." He put a hand to her cheek with a gentleness that had Lia's throat tightening.

Because if Dani was here, so hurt, where was Sammy?

A little moan escaped Dani's mouth, but she didn't open her eyes. She needed medical attention.

How were they going to manage that? They could hardly leave until they found Sammy, but…

"We'll carry her out of here," Gard said, his voice tight. He exhaled and it was shaky too. "I'll carry her to my truck."

"I'll call 911. I'll…"

"No. Dispatch will have to go by the book. We can't risk an ambulance coming down here. Not until we find Sammy. I'll carry her."

Lia happened to agree, but looking down at the incredibly injured Dani, she was torn. The woman needed a hospital, and if she didn't get help, Gard would blame himself if something terrible happened. But Sammy…

"Sammy." Dani's voice was kind of slurred and her eyes fluttered opened. They landed on Gard, though they were pained and unfocused. "Gard. Where's Sammy?" she asked, sounding less slurred, but more panicked.

"You saw her last, Dani. You tell us," Gard said. His voice was hard, but Lia knew that was to keep out the turmoil of emotion no doubt swamping him. That *hard* was the only armor keeping him together.

Dani shook her head, then moaned, lifting a hand to her head. Lia stopped her by grasping the woman's wrist, because the gash was nasty and touching it would only introduce more problems.

Dani's gaze turned to her. "Who are you? A cop?"

"I'm going to carry you back to my truck," Gard said, ignoring Dani's question to Lia. "I know it's probably going to hurt, but we're going to get you to a doctor. Don't touch your head and just hold on to me if you can."

He carefully pulled her into his arms and gingerly got to

his feet. Dani didn't really hold on to him. She was limp in his arms. Had she lost consciousness again? That wouldn't be good. She needed to stay with it.

"Dani, where are they keeping you?" Lia asked. Both to keep Dani engaged and because… Gard might have to take Dani to safety, but that didn't mean Lia had to. If Dani could tell her the holding place, Lia could go and… Find Sammy.

They had to find Sammy.

Dani groaned, her head lolling as Gard began to walk. But after a few moments, she spoke. "It's a…cellar thing. Under the barn. The barn's falling down, but the cellar is intact. They lock us up in there when they're not…" She trailed off.

Lia wasn't sure if she'd lost consciousness or didn't want to say. Particularly in front of her brother. Who was carrying her gingerly back the way he and Lia had come. Lia looked back out into the dark night. Where was the barn? Where was Sammy?

"Gard, I tried to stop them," Dani said, her voice going squeaky. "I tried so hard. They have her. In the house. You have to get her. You have to."

Sammy. Lia looked toward the house, her brain already working through options. Sammy was in the house. In the party. Lia and Gard wouldn't be able to sneak her out, but…

But Lia might be able to. If she walked into a situation she'd been in before, knew how to work.

"We'll get her. First, you need some help." Gard was walking forward, but he paused and looked over his shoulder at Lia when she didn't follow. "Come on. We'll get her to the truck and then you can drive her to the hospital. It'll be faster than waiting for an ambulance to get out this way."

But that wasn't the right plan. Lia couldn't tell if Gard

knew that and was in denial or he really hadn't thought it through.

"Gard, I need you to let me do this. You take Dani to the hospital. I'll handle this."

"I'm not leaving you here, Lia." He said it so quickly she knew he wasn't in denial. He just didn't want her doing this.

But she had to. She understood his reticence. He was the trained professional. But *she* had done this before. *She* knew how to handle this. "I promise. I know what I'm doing."

"So do I, Lia. I have a gun. I have the training. Now, come on." He started walking again, but Lia couldn't follow.

"No. Because I know how to walk into a group like this without putting up one red flag. I can walk in there and walk out *with* Sammy. I know I can. You can't go in, guns blazing. I can go in and…do what I did all those years ago. Infiltrate."

"Lia, you can't—"

"Listen to me. We don't have time to argue. I just go up to the door. I'll say Dani gave me the address. That we worked together at the diner. I'll make up a sob story and say I need a job too."

"Lia."

He sounded so absolutely wrecked, but if she thought about that, about what they were all putting him through, she might crumble. And she couldn't. Not when Sammy was in there.

"If Sammy is in there like Dani said, I get her out. I *know* I can do it. I'll sneak her out, then Royal can pick us up. He's on his way, you said. And if Sammy's not in there, I get information and walk out just fine. I know how. If you go in there, even if you take down a few guys, you get shot before you accomplish *anything*. You have to let me do this. For Sammy."

"Gard. They took Sammy in there. You have to get her out," Dani said, her voice sounding thready. Then she let out a little sob. "I tried so hard to keep her out of it."

"And if everything goes to hell? If it isn't like what you knew before? What then, Lia?"

She couldn't acknowledge any of those possibilities. She had to only focus on one thing. "I can do this," Lia said earnestly. "I *have* to do this."

Gard inhaled loudly in the quiet, freezing night. She could *feel* the way this was tearing him in two. It was tearing her in two as well, since she didn't want to hurt him any more than he was already hurting.

But they didn't have a choice.

"You will stay right here while I get Dani to the hospital. Do not go inside, not until Royal texts you that he's here. Then you can go in, and he can step in if something goes wrong. But you have to wait until he gets here."

"Yeah, okay."

"Promise?" he demanded.

Lia hesitated. Then did something that broke her heart but had to be done. She lied. "I promise."

He hesitated, but only for another few seconds. "Be safe, Lia," he said gruffly, then was walking away.

"You too," she whispered, staying where she was. His shadow disappeared quickly because of how dark it was. She wanted to rush to the house, but she waited longer than she wanted to. She didn't want him to even suspect she wouldn't wait for backup.

If this was anything like her experience, Sammy was… okay. For now. Maybe whoever had taken her inside had convinced her to take some drugs or get drunk. Maybe they'd…

No, she wouldn't go down the route of all those maybes.

In her experiences, groups like this eased into these things, because they didn't want problems. They wanted people beholden, so they wouldn't run away and cause complications for the group. They wanted and preyed on desperation. Especially these fringe type groups that were more stopping points than the big guns.

Sammy wasn't the kind to be scared into behaving the way they wanted, but they'd no doubt use Dani against her, just as they'd no doubt used Dani to get *to* her. They'd probably told Sammy she had to do things to keep her mom safe. Just like they'd probably told Dani she had to do things to keep Sammy safe.

But no one was safe. Clearly. Dani was hurt—and she hadn't done those injuries to herself. Someone had hurt her and left her there. Maybe to die.

So Lia had to act. Once she was convinced Gard was far enough away, she crept back toward the house. She couldn't possibly wait for Royal to get here, but she wasn't going to be reckless.

Not unless she saw a way to get Sammy out via recklessness.

She took her time, picking her way through the front yard, around piles of junk, and up to the porch. She carefully climbed over the broken and splintered porch stairs to leverage herself onto the warped porch boards. Light came from the house, but Lia stuck to the shadows as best she could. Sometimes the boards creaked under her feet, but there was so much noise going on inside, she didn't think anyone could possibly hear it.

She moved around broken and warped boards and shards of glass on the porch and toward one of the windows. If she got an idea of what was going on inside *before* she went inside, she might have a better plan.

The big front window was broken, but she could see through some of the spiderweb cracks. Inside, people were visible. Drinking. Shooting up. Laughing. Not one of them was paying any mind to what was going on outside the house.

Then everything inside Lia stopped, because she saw Sammy's dark hair with the blond roots. Lia could just make out her profile. Her face was red and puffy from crying, but she wasn't actively crying. Her arms were at an odd angle behind her, which lead Lia to believe she was tied up even though Lia couldn't see for sure from her vantage point.

It was both horror that she was here and relief that she was here and in one piece. Not *safe*, but not visibly *hurt* like Dani.

There was a guy standing next to Sammy holding a plastic cup, and he leaned down to say something in her ear that made Sammy grimace and lean away from him. But the man grinned like he liked that response.

Fear and fury twined inside Lia, a dangerous combination. She tried to breathe through the emotions and *focus*, but she knew she had to get inside. Now.

She moved for the door. Laughter and shouts and the murmur of voices spilled out of the house, but Lia knocked, already planning her greeting in her mind. She was a friend of Dani's. Sad and in desperate need of help.

She could make that believable. She knew what desperate felt like, deep in her bones.

When nothing happened, she knocked again, louder this time. When no one came to the door, she inhaled carefully. She knew what she had to do.

She turned the knob and pushed the door open. A few people turned toward her as she stepped inside, but a lot of people didn't even notice. There were little groups. People sitting on the floor, on tables, on furniture that was water damaged and molding. The group consisted of mostly men, but a few women were here and there—every last one of them looked high.

Lia's gaze moved to Sammy, who did indeed have her hands tied behind her back. She had that belligerent set to her chin, and all the evidence of having cried, but she otherwise seemed whole and in one piece.

But Lia couldn't stare at her. It would ruin everything.

Slowly, the talk and laughter in the room died down, and just about everyone was looking at Lia standing in the doorway. Even Sammy. But Lia couldn't meet Sammy's gaze, because there was a man with his hand around the back of Sammy's neck possessively and if Lia looked too hard at that she might blow *everything*.

So Lia looked around at the curious faces studying her. She adopted her best unsure, nervous expression. "Um, hi," she said, eyes darting around like she didn't know who to land on. "I… I was looking for a girl named Dani," she announced to the crowd.

The man who'd had his hands on Sammy, pushed away from her and took a few steps toward Lia. He studied Lia with cold, critical eyes.

"What do you want Dani for?"

"I worked with Dani at the diner." Lia kept her gaze on the man, even though she ached to rush over to Sammy. She was pretty sure this guy was the leader—if not of the whole group, at least of tonight's activities. The way everyone turned their attention toward him, like they hung on his every word, made it clear he had some kind of power or leadership here.

"She said she had a good thing going here," Lia said. She licked her lips nervously—both a little put on and very true. She leaned into the nervous—just like Agent Wood had once instructed her to do.

Don't fight your real feelings. Use them for what you need to project.

"And I just got kicked out of my boyfriend's place," Lia said, trying to make her voice shake to go along with her fake sob story. "So I just thought…maybe you'd still be looking for people, but I can leave if I'm not…welcome." She even took a step backward, toward the door.

Not that she'd ever leave Sammy, but Lia knew how to act, how to set a scene. She was practically trained by the FBI.

The man cocked his head, narrowed his eyes. Not so much in suspicion, but a slow, uncomfortable perusal.

"We're real…particular about who we hire," he said. But his mouth curved in what she figured he thought was a kind smile. Hell, maybe she would have fallen for fake kindness all those years ago.

Lia nodded like she understood *particular.* "I'm willing to work hard. I'm… I'm kind of desperate." She let the tears she was feeling over Sammy being in the middle of this pool in her eyes, then worked hard to blink them back.

Because men who did this kind of thing *loved* desperate, but they wanted a woman who was trying to be brave.

So they could break her.

Case in point. This *leader* now made a considering noise. Then he opened his arms as if in welcome. "You have come to the right place, sweetheart. We *do* need help. Now, what's your name?"

"Eddy." It's what she'd gone by way back when, so why not? She grimaced like she was embarrassed. "Pretty sure my parents were high when they handed that one out."

The guy laughed. She was even more certain he was the

ringleader when a couple other guys around him laughed too, but only after he did.

"Good one," he said with a wink. Everything he did was meant to make her at ease, but she could see all the cracks in it. The predatory gleam.

Was she just older and wiser that she didn't fall for it, or had her captors way back when just been that much more charismatic? And did it matter? She'd been fifteen and desperate.

She wasn't any more. She was here to save Sammy. That was all that mattered.

"Speaking of high, what's your poison?" He swept his hand around the room. Most people had gone back to whatever they'd been doing, but a few of the men were watching her with intent eyes.

She didn't even try to hide her nerves. It was expected. Hell, they probably fed off it.

"You're going to…share?" Lia asked somewhat skeptically. Then she let out a nervous laugh. "That's not really a good sign in my experience."

"Oh, don't be suspicious, Eddy. We're all family here. If you join the family, you get *all* the perks of the family. We take care of our own. There's some good stuff here." He pointed at a table where some needles and other items Lia didn't recognize sat.

Luckily, Lia had spent most of her teen years making excuses not to partake. She knew how to avoid and deflect. "Needles make me nervous. I wouldn't mind a drink though."

"Sure, sweetheart. You just come with me." The man slung his arm around her shoulders in an overfriendly move. Lia worked hard not to stiffen as he pulled her deeper into the house.

She glanced at Sammy on her way past, just couldn't resist. Sammy was watching her with wide, scared eyes. Lia did her best to force a reassuring smile.

Everything was going to be okay. She was going to make sure of it.

Chapter Seventeen

Gard managed to carry Dani back to his truck. The physical exertion helped keep his mind off of Lia going in *there*. He'd needed to use every ounce of strength to make it to the truck without dropping Dani.

Once at his truck, he managed to lay Dani out in the back seat. She wasn't lucid. Sometimes she'd have some clarity, but then she'd just start crying about Sammy or mumbling things Gard couldn't understand. But she stayed conscious, and that was important. Conscious was alive.

She desperately needed medical attention though, so he could hardly leave her here to go back to Lia and Sammy, but… How could he leave them?

I can do this. I have to do this. Lia had been so earnest when she'd said that, so determined. And this was all for Sammy. And Dani.

So he had to think like a cop. Not like the terrified man he was, being pulled in too many different directions. Because fear couldn't get them out of this, but his training could. Lia's understanding of the situation could.

So, the plan had to change a little. Gard couldn't possibly leave Lia here, so when Royal arrived, *he* should take Dani into the hospital. So Gard could go back and handle this.

He got into the driver's side of his truck, pulling out his phone.

Dani was crying faintly, but that meant she was alive and breathing, so Gard tried to harden his heart to the sound and focus on what needed to be done. If he handed Dani off to Royal, *he* could get back to Lia.

He didn't love the idea of Dani feeling like she was being passed off to a man she didn't know that well, but there was no way Gard was able to get through this if he had to drive Dani all the way to the hospital. Besides, it would keep Royal from having to be on the hook for any trouble anyway.

He dialed Royal, who answered almost immediately.

"Hey. I'm just about there. Just turning into Wilde. What's up?"

"Okay. Stop at the intersection of Dry and the highway." He hadn't realized how out of breath he was from carrying Dani until he tried to talk clearly. "I'll meet you there in a minute and explain everything."

Formulating the plan as he drove the short distance, he arrived at the meeting point just about the time Royal did.

Gard got out of his truck and Royal followed suit, meeting him between the hoods of their trucks.

"I need you to take my truck," Gard told Royal. "My sister is in the back seat. She's hurt. She needs a hospital. You take her to the ER and get her the medical attention she needs. I'll be there as soon as I can."

"What are you going to do?"

"Sammy and Lia are still in that house. I'm going to get them out."

"You let a *civilian* go in there?" Royal said, clearly both shocked and disapproving.

"Lia knows what she's doing. Let's switch keys," he said,

holding his out to Royal, but Royal clearly hadn't clued into just how little time they had.

"How the hell does Lia the *bakery owner* know what she's doing when it comes to some criminal organization?"

But Gard didn't have time to answer that question. He tried to hand Royal his keys again, but they were both distracted by another truck pulling up.

"That's Zeke and his brother, Walker," Royal said. "Their sister is stepmom to one of your niece's friends, so they kind of already have the gist of what's going on," Royal explained. "How many people are in that house?"

"At least ten. Probably more. Probably armed."

"Probably," Royal muttered disgustedly. "Let's do it this way. Walker will drive your sister to the hospital. Zeke and I will come with you. Between the three of us, we should be able to handle over ten guys."

"Ten guys?" Zeke said on approach. "Piece of cake."

Gard appreciated the confidence, even if it didn't penetrate. He handed his truck keys to Walker, then moved to his truck. He opened the back door to talk to his sister.

"Dani, a friend of mine is going to drive you to the hospital. You're safe with him, I promise. I'm going to go get Sammy."

She looked up at him with tears in eyes glazed over with pain. Her face was so bloody. Everything was so *bad*. "Gard."

"Let the doctors take care of you," he said, managing to keep his voice firm instead of hoarse. "I'll bring Sammy to you as soon as I can." He pressed a gentle kiss to her forehead. "Be good." He closed the door, not waiting to see if she was going to say anything else.

One person was safe now.

He just had to get the other two.

THE RINGLEADER, who called himself Bruiser, had insisted Lia take a seat at a kitchen table that had seen better days. The wind howled in through the broken window in the kitchen area and Lia shivered against the cold.

Whatever Bruiser was on must have been keeping him warm because he only wore a frayed T-shirt and ratty jeans that looked like they hadn't been washed in a while. He was making her a drink. She figured he thought he was slick since she couldn't see what he was putting in it.

And she supposed he was slick enough. Ten years ago, she would have fallen for it hook, line and sinker instead of recognizing the hunched posture, the carefully arranged body to block anything he was doing from her line of vision.

So when he put the cup in front of her, she smiled tremulously at him, trying to remember who she'd been and what she'd felt at fifteen. She needed him to believe it. The fear, desperation, and sad, pathetic hope *someone* might save her.

He slid into the rickety chair next to her. Like, *right* next to her. Lia had to fight the urge to lean away. Not out of fear. Just pure disgust.

Don't fight your real feelings. Use them for what you need to project. So Lia let her body hold that wariness and fought the disgust from showing in her expression.

They were alone in this room, though she could look out into the living room and see Sammy. The girl sat stiffly on a table, arms tied behind her back with a frayed-looking rope. No one went up to talk to her or bother her, which was good considering the circumstances, Lia supposed.

But Lia had a bad feeling that meant she was earmarked for somebody. Probably the man currently talking to *her.*

Maybe it was something about being so much older now that even though she was worried about how she was going to get Sammy out of this, she wasn't *scared*. Because she wasn't desperate. Soon enough, she'd have backup.

And she'd done this before, and on a much bigger scale. This was, as JJ would have said all those years ago, small-time. The bottom rung of something much, much bigger no doubt, but in the here and now? Nothing compared to what she'd brought down before.

When she'd had *no one*. Now? She had too many people on her side, in her corner. And so did Sammy.

"So, how'd you get here?" Bruiser asked, his arm brushing against hers. "We didn't hear any cars pull up."

Lia considered pointing out they hadn't even heard her knock, but it was probably smarter not to correct him. She tried to stay close to the truth without telling all of it, in case he tried to verify her story.

"My boyfriend wrecked my car a while back, so I don't have any transportation. I had to walk all the way out here. When I said I was desperate, I wasn't exaggerating. My boyfriend kicked me out and I don't have a damn thing or person to turn to." She pretended to take a deep gulp of the drink. She was pretty sure he'd put something in it, so she was going to have to find a way to pour some of it out when he wasn't looking.

She also needed to find a way to get his attention elsewhere so she could get to Sammy and get her out of there.

Bruiser was watching her intently, so Lia kept on with the story. Pretending like she couldn't help but overshare.

"We were living over in Wilde, so it wasn't too long of a walk. I…didn't really have anywhere else to go. My family doesn't want anything to do with me. Dani was like, my only friend. I haven't seen her in a while though. Does she still work for you guys?"

"Oh, yeah. One of our top workers," Bruiser said, his

eyes on her drink so Lia had to pretend to take another sip. When she put the cup back down, she tried to casually rest her hand over the top so he couldn't tell she hadn't actually drunk any.

"Um, I hope you don't mind me asking, but uh…" Lia leaned forward, going for conspiratorial. She pointed in Sammy's direction. "Why is that girl tied up?"

"Oh. Don't worry about that. Nothing criminal." He laughed, far too loud in her ear. He leaned closer, so she could feel his breath on her cheek and allowed the shudder to move through her. He could interpret it however he liked, and she knew he wouldn't see it for the revulsion it was.

"She likes it."

Lia wanted to vomit, but she managed not to grimace at the horrifying words.

"Um, well." She laughed nervously, because it fit the character she was playing. And she used this as an excuse to try to make her first escape. If she could convince him she was too skittish, grab Sammy before he went back into the living room… It was worth a shot.

"I'm not… I don't think…" She put her hands on the table and shoved herself up to her feet. She pretended to sway a little so he thought she was affected by whatever he put in the drink. So he didn't see her as a threat. "Maybe I should go."

His hand clamped on her wrist. "Where ya' going, Eddy? If you're desperate, you can't be too good for a job, can you?" His grip was hard, the light in his eyes mean. But he kept his mouth curved, like that sharp, predatory smile would be some kind of comfort.

Whether he meant to or not, he was working both sides of it—trying to *appear* friendly and helpful, but also a little threatening. So she'd be lost, confused, off-balance.

Yeah, he meant to.

Lia blinked, trying to work on getting a tear to slip over so he didn't see the flash of rage that moved through her. She was almost certain she could knock him over—just one well-placed elbow to the throat.

But that didn't get her and Sammy out of here. And he wasn't going to let her go easy, so she had to adjust. How to get Sammy out without Lia grabbing her and pulling her out? "No, I'm not too good, but…"

A shout sounded out in the living room, and Lia could see two guys pushing and shoving each other. There were some shouts, some cheers.

Bruiser sighed irritably. "Just stay here. Enjoy your drink. There's still a little interview process to go once I take care of this." He made no bones about staring down her shirt as he got up, but Lia pretended not to notice. She pretended to be shocked by the fighting going on out in the living room.

So Bruiser swaggered over to where the two men were fighting. He gave one a hard push away from the other. The not-pushed guy started laughing while the other was clearly trying to get the crowd of people on his side. Bruiser must have been the decider of who won, because they both appealed to him.

While he handled that, Lia got up out of her chair. Casually, or at least she hoped casually, she ambled into the living room. Like she was interested in the fight and what Bruiser's decision would be.

But instead of heading toward Bruiser, she moved to Sammy, resting a hip against the table Sammy was sitting on. Lia held the cup up to her mouth, her eyes on the fighters, so no one would immediately notice she was even speaking to Sammy.

Because the fight gave her just the idea she needed.

"I'm going to create a diversion," Lia said quietly. "When I do, you're not going to run. You're just going to get up and walk out the front door. Calm. Easy. Don't look back."

"Lia." Sammy's voice was hoarse. Terrified.

Lia kept her gaze on Bruiser, swallowed down any emotional response to Sammy's fear. "That's all you have to do. Walk out the front door, down the drive. Gard or a police officer will be waiting for you. We've got your mom. You just need to get out."

"What about you?" Sammy demanded.

Lia ignored her and got to her feet, wandering back to the kitchen like she was just taking in the scenery.

She had to think of a diversion. Something that would bring everyone running.

When she saw the lighter on the counter, she knew just what to do.

Chapter Eighteen

Lia looked around for the most flammable part of the kitchen. There was a door, presumably out to the backyard, that was all splintered wood. Would it be dry enough to go up in flames if she got the lighter in the right spot? Probably not, but what about something more sustained than just the lighter?

She glanced back at the living room where Bruiser currently had one of the fighters in what seemed to be a good-natured headlock, while a couple people cheered.

Perfect. In quick, efficient moves, Lia grabbed a dirty old dishrag from the sink. It was crusty and dry. Would alcohol help it start on fire? She wasn't sure, so she didn't go that route. She just grabbed the lighter and moved to the door. She leaned against it, trying to look casual—the lighter and rag hidden behind the chair that was in front of her.

She looked out at the living room. The headlock was over, but Bruiser hadn't made his way to her yet. He was messing with Sammy now.

Lia resisted the urge to run interference. Distraction first. Trying to look as casual as possible, she flicked the lighter on and tried to light the dirty rag. It took a while to catch fire, then immediately went out when she tried to drop it by the door.

She went through the process again, always keeping an eye on Bruiser. He was making the rounds, talking to people. He touched every single woman in the room in some familiar way—a hand down their hair, their arm, a squeeze on the knee, or even a few times very affectionate hugs.

Most of the women seemed to be using more than interested, but they were all outnumbered by the men who clearly looked at Bruiser as the leader.

The second time Lia managed to get the rag on fire, she carefully crouched and placed it next to the splintered door. She watched it try to catch on the door.

Please. Please. Please.

She glanced up and Bruiser was back with Sammy. Lia had to fight against the lick of scalding fury that erupted inside of her at his hand on the back of Sammy's neck.

They were running out of time. She needed this fire to *catch*. To do what it needed to do. Lia moved back over to the kitchen counter, grabbed a bottle of vodka. Then she carefully poured a few dribbles into the flames, causing them to shoot higher. She splashed a little more across the wood of the door, hoping it would accelerate the fire.

Once satisfied with that, she put the vodka back on the counter. She didn't look back at the fire now. She moved closer to the living room for some plausible deniability.

She knew she shouldn't watch Bruiser and Sammy intently, but she couldn't help it. His mouth was at her ear, clearly saying something to her, but it was all getting a little too close.

When he *accidentally*—as in, not at all accidentally— spilled his drink down Sammy's shirtfront, causing Sammy to yelp in surprise, Lia couldn't wait for the fire to catch any bigger.

She had to act.

"There's a fire!" Lia shouted, stumbling out of the kitchen. She wished it would catch more, but this was enough of a distraction.

She hoped.

Someone screamed, while a couple of the guys rushed forward—including Bruiser. Lia carefully moved out of the way, but didn't escape the kitchen. She wanted Sammy out first.

More people crowded around, but Lia craned her neck to see around them. Sammy was still sitting on the table, and their gazes caught.

Lia gave the girl a nod. Inwardly, she urged her to move. Go. While everyone was distracted. When Sammy just stood there, Lia mouthed the words.

Go. Now.

Finally Sammy stood, then took a step toward the door, then another. Her hands were still tied, so when she got to the door, she backed toward it, having to open it behind her back. But she pulled it open.

No one noticed. Everyone was shouting things to do about the fire. Everyone's focus was on the kitchen.

Sammy gave Lia one last pleading look, there in the door opening, but Lia shook her head. *Go.*

Lia held her breath until Sammy disappeared into the dark. Then she let it out in a slow, careful exhale. Now she just needed to get herself out.

She stepped away from the crowd, turned her back to them. Slowly. Casually. She didn't look at anyone. She kept her chin high, so it looked like she knew what she was doing and like she *should* be doing it.

She was nearly at the door, had even reached out to grab the knob.

But then something caught her from behind and jerked her back. An arm came around her throat.

"I'm going to kill you, Eddy," she heard Bruiser seethe as the pressure on her windpipe increased and she struggled to breathe.

But he didn't go after Sammy or send anyone else after her, so it was okay.

No matter what happened, it was okay, because she'd gotten Sammy out.

Royal parked his truck in the ditch closer to the driveway than Gard had originally been. With the partying going on, Gard didn't think it was too much of a risk to drive this close, and it got them back to the house quicker.

He hopped out, already moving forward as Royal and Zeke trailed behind. "I don't know how many weapons they've got," he told them. "Drugs are a certainty, and many of them are probably high, which makes them volatile and unpredictable. We know Sammy is in that house. Lia should be waiting for us outside, but we don't know if any other people are being held against their will, so we have to be careful."

Three armed men against an unknown number of highly erratic targets. Not exactly the best situation. But it didn't have to be a full-on fight. If he could get Sammy out of that house with stealth, all the better.

They walked up the drive, the house in sight. Gard studied the dark shadows of the yard where he'd left Lia but didn't see anything that looked like it might be a person. He pulled his phone out of his pocket and typed in a text.

Where are you?

He waited for an answer, but none came. Frustrated and worried, he considered the house. The situation. Surely she hadn't gone in there alone before she'd gotten a text from Royal... Surely she hadn't broken her promise.

But he had a sinking suspicion that's just what she'd done.

He shook it away. Sammy *was* in there, or Lia would have gotten a message to him. So that meant *he* had to get in there. And if Lia was in there too... Well, they'd deal with that.

Maybe it hadn't been the deal, but... Lia knew what she was doing. He had to trust that she knew what she was getting herself into. If there was something to be mad about, he'd save that anger for when they were all safe.

"There are two entrances," he told Zeke and Royal. "Here in the front, and then in the back. When I was here a few weeks ago, the back door was grown over with vines, so I'm not sure it's a viable entrance point."

"If we can get through the vines without anyone noticing, could be a surprise entrance point," Zeke said. "And with that music playing, I think you could probably cut through enough to get a door open without anyone noticing."

"If it's not locked," Royal offered.

"Clearly they're not too worried about being snuck up on," Zeke replied. "Even if it's locked, it'd be easy enough to pick and get in there. Probably without anyone noticing. Whatever they're up to right now, they're not worried about being caught."

Zeke wasn't wrong, though it was still a risk and dangerous because drugs made people unpredictable. But they had to get in there. "You two go around back and see what you can accomplish."

"What are you going to do? Walk in the front?" Royal demanded.

"Yeah. Why not?"

"Because I've had the same training you have, Gard. Training *you* gave me, if you'll recall. I get that it's different because your niece is inside, but that training *is* to keep everyone as safe as possible. No training we've ever gone through says *Hey, walk in the front door of a volatile situation alone*."

Maybe Royal was right, but Gard didn't have to like it. "I can keep an eye on things through the window. You guys see what you can do in the back. I'll only go in if I have to."

Royal clearly didn't love that answer, but Gard needed them to *go*. "If we have a way out back, we can sneak Sammy and Lia out that way. Get it open. I'll make sure no one comes out the front. Come on. Move."

Royal finally relented and he and Zeke moved away from Gard, melting into the shadows.

Gard put them out of his mind as he studied the house. He couldn't waltz in the front, no. But he could get a better view of what was going on inside. A head count. He could make a visual on Sammy, on Lia if she was in there. Formulate a plan.

Maybe he could even create some kind of diversion. If he could get all these people pouring out of the house, maybe in the chaos he could get to Sammy and Lia. Get them away from this without any confrontation Sammy had to witness.

But he needed more information first, which meant getting closer. Careful to stay in the shadows, he started to move. Listening to the sounds of the party, paying attention to the world around him.

He frowned a little as an odd smell filled the air. He couldn't quite pick it out while his mind focused on getting to Sammy. On where Lia might be.

A few yards from the porch, his phone buzzed in his pocket, momentarily distracting him from his target. Laurel's name was on the screen when he pulled it out, so he answered, hoping for news on the warrant.

"Fairhurst," he answered in a quiet voice, not taking his eyes off the shadows moving inside the house, making sure no one took interest in what was going on outside in the frigid cold.

"We've got a search warrant for the house," Laurel said without preamble. "Still working on the property beyond the house. They're owned by two different people."

"I got Dani. I sent her with Walker Daniels to the hospital. She told me they're keeping people in a cellar under a barn. You have an eyewitness. Get the warrant. And get a team out here."

Laurel was quiet for a few seconds—but he could hear the hum of voices. Like she'd covered her receiver and was barking out orders.

"Beckett is on his way to Dry Road. He'll be waiting for the search warrant to come through with some deputies. I'll call again about it, then head to the hospital to talk to Dani."

"She might not be up for it," Gard said, hoping it wasn't true but needing to prepare Laurel for the possibility.

"Okay. I'll see what I can do with it. Please tell me you haven't pulled in any civilians besides Walker Daniels."

But Gard could *not* tell her that. Though technically Royal wasn't a civilian, and Zeke didn't *seem* like a civilian.

Laurel sighed heavily. "How many, Fairhurst? Just so I can tell Beckett and he doesn't try to arrest your civilian help."

Wincing, Gard realized he had to give over the names. "Royal Campbell and Zeke Daniels. They aren't doing anything. They're just…backup."

"Sure," Laurel replied. "Listen. We've got movement. We'll have people on standby, ready to move the second we can. Just sit tight."

Sit tight? No, he didn't think so.

Gard looked at the house and since he wasn't thinking so damn hard about what was going on in there, it finally dawned on him what the odd smell stinging his nostrils was.

Smoke. And from somewhere behind the house, he saw a flicker of light…flame. Fire.

So no, he couldn't sit tight. The house was on *fire*.

"Call the fire department, Laurel," he barked into the phone, then shoved it into his pocket.

And ran.

Chapter Nineteen

Gard was at the bottom of the pile of what had once been porch stairs when the door creaked open. He froze in his quick rush toward the house, determined to get to Sammy and Lia before any *fire* did.

A shadow moved out onto the porch, slowly and carefully. One step back and then another. Then the person turned into the light coming out of the window.

"Sammy." Fire forgotten, Gard rushed toward her.

She let out a desperate kind of sound. "Gard." She fell into him at a kind of awkward angle, clearly not seeing that there were no stairs. But he caught her, and she was sobbing into his chest as held her close.

Relief swamped him, but he couldn't let that make him forget there was still danger here. He started to carry her away from the house. He'd gotten her into the shadows as a couple other people stumbled out of the house and onto the porch, clearly in response to the fire. Some were coughing. Some were complaining about the party being ruined.

Quickly and quietly as he could, Gard carried Sammy through the shadows, as far away from the people as he could. Her arms were behind her back, and he couldn't quite figure out why, but he didn't want to ask her until he had her out of earshot of the people trickling out from the house.

Once he had carried her into a thicket of overgrown bushes, keeping them in shadow and hidden even if people started using flashlights, he spoke.

"Can you walk? Are you hurt?"

"I… I'm okay," Sammy said on a choked sob. "But they hurt Mom. They hurt her and left her outside. Lia said you got her, but—"

"We've got her. She's on her way to the hospital. She's going to be okay."

Sammy made another sobbing noise. "My…my hands are tied up," she managed to say, clearly trying to whisper but struggling.

Gard couldn't see in the dark, but he felt down her arms then gently turned her in place so he could try to untie the knots even in the dark. His hands fumbled on the ties. Lia hadn't come out of that house yet, and he had to get to her, but Sammy needed to get out of here. Fully out of here.

Surely Lia would come out with the other group of people. She wasn't just going to stick around in a fire.

Unless.

Gard shoved that *unless* away and focused on untying Sammy.

He heard the sound of approaching footsteps. Careful footsteps. Gard let out a low whistle, a signal to Royal or Zeke if it was them. He couldn't see in the dark, but he knew it was them when they nearly silently entered the thicket of bushes.

"One of you get me a light, the other hide it as best you can. I have to get her untied."

Some shuffling and then the light of one of their phones clicked on at a very low setting, but enough Gard could see the knots and fully untie them.

"Gard, Lia is still in there. With him," Sammy said. Her

voice was scratchy but she sounded more determined than scared. "She set the fire to get me out. But she wouldn't come with me. She stayed there. With *him*."

Gard looked at the house. People milled in the yard now. Some laughed. Some shouted. The fire had grown in intensity but was still relegated to the backside of the house. He searched the crowd again. Even though it was shadowy, he thought he'd be able to recognize Lia.

She wasn't among them, or she'd be separating herself. She'd be trying to find them. She'd be doing *something*.

"Still in there with who?" Gard asked.

"I don't know. Mom knows. He's the guy who hurt her. He hit Mom so hard and…" Sammy started to sob again.

"It's okay, baby. I've almost got it." He fumbled a little more, but finally got the knots undone so Sammy's hands fell to her sides. He pulled her into a hug, tight and close. Relief coursed through him, twined with the continued worry for Lia.

Lia. He had to get her out of there. But first… Sammy…

"Could you guys get in the back of the house?" Gard asked Royal and Zeke in low tones.

"No. Cut through the overgrowth on the door just fine, but the fire started right there by the door. Blocking any entrance or exit from the back. We could see in the kitchen window—the fire is basically *on* the door."

Gard swore inwardly, rubbing his hands up and down Sammy's arms to try and keep her warm. He wished he had a coat for her, but he didn't have anything. He'd need Royal and Zeke to take her to the truck, and Gard would go find Lia and—

"Gard, like I said, we could see through a window," Royal said carefully. Too carefully. "A guy was…holding Lia in the kitchen. Right by the fire."

Gard's grip on Sammy tightened for a second before he forced himself to relax his hands. It was his only outward reaction. Inwardly, he didn't let himself have a reaction either. He just relied on his training. He knew how to deal with danger, emergencies, threats.

He'd deal with this one.

He crouched a little so he could be eye level with Sammy. "I need you to go with Deputy Campbell, okay? He's a police officer and a good friend of mine. You do what he says. You can trust him. I promise." He moved her toward Royal. "Get her out of here. I'm going to go get Lia."

"But…"

The protests came from Sammy *and* Royal, but Gard ignored them. "It's all right. Everything is going to be okay."

Trusting Royal to take care of Sammy, Gard stepped out of the bushes and headed for the house.

Because he was damn well going to make sure of it.

LIA STRUGGLED AGAINST the too-tight grip on her throat. Every once in a while, she managed to take in a breath when Bruiser's grip loosened a little bit.

But mostly she wasn't getting nearly enough oxygen, which made panic scatter through her. The panic was making her sloppy as Bruiser dragged her back toward the fire.

He'd ordered everyone else outside, so it was just him and her now. And the fire he was dragging her toward.

"You want to ruin my place?" he demanded. "You'll get ruined in return."

She tried to pull against his grip on her throat, dig her heels in so he couldn't keep dragging her forward. There'd been a time when she'd known how to fight back—or if not fight back, mitigate the painful results. Seven years of safety had made her soft. Panic was dulling her instincts.

Think. What would Agent Wood say? She tried to think back the FBI Agent who'd given her the skills to bring down an entire *group* of criminals.

When you're in a tough spot, you look for the weak spot.

Bruiser was strong, no doubt aided by fury and whatever he was on. The grip on her neck tightened until she started to see spots. She needed to breathe. She needed air.

Don't panic. Weak spot. Weak spot.

He was trying to drag her forward and she was fighting it. But she couldn't fight it. Surprise was a weak spot, she remembered.

So with the last bit of energy she had, she stopped fighting the forward progress and threw her weight into it instead. Bruiser stumbled in surprise now that there was no oppositional force. His grip loosened enough for her to suck in a breath as they stumbled forward, toward the fire.

But Bruiser regained his footing quick enough, and after maybe two decent breaths, his arm was crushing against her windpipe again.

They were so close to the fire now. She could feel the heat pouring off it. Flames licked higher and higher, smoke hanging in the air so that even if she could get a breath, it was sour and heavy.

"You like fire so much?" Bruiser said, huffing and puffing in the exertion of the fight. "Let's see how you like this."

Lia braced herself, or tried, for whatever he was threatening. She held her breath and planted her feet and—

"Let go of her and step away."

Both Lia and Bruiser stilled. Tears immediately filled Lia's vision. It was Gard's voice. She couldn't see him because of Bruiser's grip on her, but she *knew* it was him.

Here. To save her.

Bruiser carefully turned, but he positioned Lia in front

of him. She pulled at his arm on her windpipe because she couldn't breathe again. She didn't want Gard to see her like this, but he stood there. Stoic. Sure.

Gun pointed at them.

Smoke swirled between them as flames licked up the door and wall behind Lia and Bruiser, but she could see Gard's blue eyes were intense and direct and on Bruiser. Not on her.

After trying to save Sammy, Lia understood why. He was maintaining focus and distance because he wouldn't be able to do either if he focused on her. Just like she hadn't been able to spend time looking directly at Sammy without emotions taking over.

"Who the hell are you?" Bruiser demanded, which made sense. Gard didn't look very cop-like in his plain clothes, gun drawn, and blank expression on his face. He looked like some kind of…vigilante or something.

But he didn't answer Bruiser's question. "Drop your arm and step away or I shoot," he said, calm and intimidating.

Lia could feel Bruiser moving behind her. She didn't know what he was doing, but she could hear him messing with something. She struggled to get a little, tiny breath, but it wasn't enough. It wasn't enough. So much so she almost didn't know that Bruiser was now holding the sharp edge of something against her back.

Gard couldn't see it. He didn't know. And Lia couldn't tell him, because she couldn't even breathe.

"This is your last chance," Gard said. His finger curled around the trigger.

Lia didn't know how he could shoot when Bruiser was using her as some kind of shield, but Bruiser's grip on her neck eased a little bit. Lia could struggle in a smoke-filled breath and then another. She coughed on both, but it didn't even matter. He was letting her really breathe. She thought maybe… Maybe he was actually going to let her go fully. He was afraid enough of the gun that he would do what Gard said.

But he had a knife…or *something* sharp pointed into her back. If he let her go and Gard didn't shoot, would he hurt Gard with it instead?

Lia couldn't let that happen.

So with another sucked-in breath, she managed to get out half the sentence. "He's got a kni—" Then she let out a scream of pain as agony sliced through her.

Chapter Twenty

Lia cried out—clearly in pain, so Gard did the only thing he knew how to do. He fired his weapon at his target.

The man who'd been holding Lia fell backward, but Lia did too, falling right on top of him with another cry of pain.

Gard rushed forward, pulled Lia off of the man and into his arms and as far away from the fire as he could. He wanted to find out where she'd been hurt, carry her out of here, but he had to be sure he'd incapacitated her captor.

Trying to be gentle, he shoved her behind him, so he was between her and the man.

Who writhed on the floor, blood pouring out of his shoulder. The one part of his body he hadn't been able to hide behind Lia, making it the only target for Gard to shoot at. Fire licked around the guy, but he seemed more pained by the bullet wound.

He swore and groaned and squirmed there on the floor. He didn't appear to have a gun or any other weapon, but next to him on the floor was a knife.

Covered in blood.

He swore and whirled to Lia. She'd stumbled back into the table but was holding herself upright with one hand against it. The other hand clasped her side. Blood leaked out between her fingers.

For one horrible moment, everything inside of him froze. Instinct, training, everything evaporated and there was only a bone-deep, mind-numbing terror at the sight of Lia's blood.

"I'm okay," she said, but she said it through gritted teeth. And that poked through the freeze. Everything shuffled back into place.

Act. He had to *act*. Save.

Her gaze met his, clouded with pain, but coherent. "Sammy?"

"She's good. Now let's get you good. You need an ambulance." Gard still had the gun pointed at the man. The guy had shoved himself against the cabinets and was sitting up, cursing up a blue streak as blood oozed from his shoulder. Fire crackled around them and the smoke was getting thick enough to start to become a problem. The man's gaze was on the knife. He reached out.

In quick moves, Gard strode forward and kicked the knife far away from the man. He could feel the heat from the fire, smoke stinging his eyes and throat.

Likely the guy was going to suffer burns if he didn't get out of the way.

Gard felt nothing about that observation.

Gard moved over to Lia without looking away from the man. He couldn't carry her and hold his gun ready to shoot. He couldn't really put his arm around her waist and help her walk without hurting where she was holding herself.

"It's okay," Lia said, her voice sounding thready at best. "I can walk."

He wasn't sure he believed her, but if she could get to the front...

"Walk out the front door. Royal's brother-in-law should be waiting for you, okay? Tell him to send in someone to

arrest this asshole once backup arrives." He eyed her speculatively. "Lia…"

"I got it," she said. She was ashen at this point, but she
pushed off the table and walked out of the room, clutching
her side. Just like he'd asked her to.

The fire kept growing up the side of the door. Flames
licked the ceiling now. Gard pulled his shirt up over his
nose to try and block out some of the smoke that was making his eyes water.

"A lot of drugs for as small-time as you guys are," Gard
told the man on the floor.

He looked even paler than Lia, turning a pasty kind of
gray. "Small-time." The guy snorted. "You have no idea,
buddy."

Gard smiled at him, but it wasn't nice, though it was
hidden behind his shirt. "Good. That means we're going
to find out, and you won't see life out of a cell for a very
long time."

Gard heard sirens now. The sound of voices outside the
back door. Firemen, he hoped. He didn't want to just leave
this guy here, even with the gunshot wound, but he needed
to get to Lia and—

Beckett strode in from the front, gun drawn, badge hanging from around his neck. He surveyed the kitchen.

"Stand down, Fairhurst. Go take care of your family.
I've got it from here."

Gard gave one last look at the man who'd hurt Lia. And
Sammy. And Dani, no doubt. "Don't be gentle," he told
Beckett.

And then he was jogging outside. There was a fire truck,
and two ambulances parked outside, along with a row of
patrol cars, all with their lights flashing. The group that

had been partying was mostly being arrested, though Gard wouldn't be surprised if a few had made a run for it.

He couldn't care about that when he saw Sammy running toward him. She reached him and threw her arms around him, and he held on tight.

"You're supposed to be long gone, kid." He looked around, trying to find Lia in the crowd. She should be with the ambulances. One was pulling away. Was she in it?

"When the police cars got here, Deputy Campbell said it was okay if we stayed," Sammy said, still holding tight to him. "The paramedics wouldn't let me sit with Lia. They just took her away. What happened, Gard?"

"Come on. We'll follow to the hospital." He put his arm around her and started to lead her toward the road. "Did they check you out? Are you okay?"

"I'm fine. All those guys did was tie me up and…say awful things. They didn't hurt me though. Just Mom. Have you heard anything about Mom?"

"Not yet. Let's find Royal. He'll drive us to the hospital. We'll see everybody. It's all right now."

Gard wanted to believe it, but he wasn't sure he'd breathe until he saw Dani and Lia again. Safe and sound.

He searched the crowd for Royal, but before he could get anywhere, Laurel approached.

"Fairhurst." Her expression was calm, and she smiled reassuringly at Sammy. "I know you'd like to get to the hospital, but I'd really like to hear Sammy's side of things before I let you guys go. It'll help us deal with charges quicker if we can get it down now."

Frustrated with the holdup, but knowing this was best, Gard nodded. He squeezed Sammy to his side, and reminded himself Lia might have been bleeding, but she'd walked out of that house on her own two feet.

She was okay. They were all going to be okay. And they were going to put these assholes behind bars.

"Tell Detective Delaney-Carson everything you know, and then we'll go to the hospital. Okay? Just start from the beginning. Your mom texted you when you were at the movie?"

Sammy nodded, leaning into him. "Yeah. I knew she'd keep hounding me if I didn't go out there, or worse. Maybe she'd come in and make a scene. I knew she'd want me to go somewhere, but I didn't… I didn't *want* to. So I gave my purse to Izzy and said I had to go to the bathroom. I figured if Mom tried to get me to go somewhere with her, I'd tell her I left my purse and phone inside and I'd go get it and call you."

"That was smart, Sammy," Laurel said reassuringly. "It definitely helped us find you quicker. So you went out to the back of the movie theater?"

Sammy nodded. "I didn't see Mom, but this guy came up and grabbed me. I was fighting him—I totally kneed him in the crotch and he swore. I know I hurt him, but… He pointed to a car, and I could see Mom was in the back. They…they…" Her voice broke. "They were hurting her."

Gard held her even tighter. She was crying, but she got the rest of the story out. How she'd gone with them, so they'd stop hurting her mom. How they'd brought them both here. Tied Sammy up, beat Dani when she tried to stop them, then pretended like everything was fine and she was just invited to this party while they left Dani unconscious in the backyard.

"I kept crying, asking for Mom, but they just laughed and took me inside. I think he liked that I was crying, that I was scared. So I tried to stop…being that on the outside."

"That's brave, Sammy," Gard managed to croak out

through a throat so tight it was a wonder he could breathe. "Very brave."

"They took me inside and mostly that guy would just say…gross stuff to me, but he didn't *do* anything. He said stuff about drugs, but he didn't make me take anything or drink anything. He was going to…hurt me or do something. I know he was going to, but…he wanted to mess with me first. But then Lia came."

Tears were streaming down her face. She looked up at Gard. "She set the fire so I could get out. She saved me."

Gard nodded. He had to clear his throat to speak. "That should be enough, Laurel. We're going to the hospital. Now."

Laurel nodded. "Go with Morris. She'll run code to get you there ASAP."

Lia FELT WOOZY. She didn't think she'd done a very good job of answering the doctor's questions, and now she was waiting in a hospital gown, a big bandage fastened to her side.

Someone would come stitch her up soon. They'd already put some local anesthesia on the spot—after painfully disinfecting the hell out of it—and now they were just giving the anesthesia time to work.

Apparently, she had a bruised windpipe, but no serious damage that couldn't heal on its own there. The smoke inhalation was negligent. The stab wound had been deep and would require some serious babying, but it hadn't hit anything important enough to require surgery.

Which was all great and good, but she couldn't just sit around here, bored out of her mind, waiting. She needed information and she didn't know where her phone had gone to in the fray.

She needed to see Sammy or talk to Gard, or she'd even

settle for Royal if someone could tell her what was going *on*. She *knew* Sammy got out, but was Dani okay? Was Gard beating himself up?

She needed to know.

Carefully, she sat up in bed. Still woozy, definitely dizzy, but she could totally walk if she could hold onto something. She pushed to her feet.

It didn't hurt so much—the pain seemed to float under a cloud of something else, the painkillers—but she wasn't steady at all and her vision kind of wavered. She sat back down on the edge of the bed with a thud, and then a wince as some pain jolted past the cloud.

She sucked in a breath, let one out. She willed herself to find some equilibrium. On a careful breath she got to her feet again—just as the door moved and someone slipped inside, quickly closing it behind them.

Sammy.

"What the hell do you think you're doing?" she demanded of Lia, storming over to the bed. "You shouldn't stand up. Get right back into that bed." She fisted one hand on one hip and pointed the other at the bed.

She looked very adult and…*fine*. Just safe and good and fine. Lia's eyes filled with tears. Okay. Safe. Sound. But she didn't want Sammy to worry about *her*.

"Yes, nurse," Lia managed to croak out through a tight throat, just drinking in how *okay* Sammy seemed. Ordering her around. Not a scratch on her. Lia blinked the tears away as she sat back down on the bed. "What are *you* doing here?"

Sammy's expression went sheepish. "I'm not supposed to be here. I caused a big scene and then…snuck in." She shrugged. "That distraction technique works, huh?"

Lia catalogued every feature. She was wearing different clothes than she had been, but she clearly hadn't showered or anything because her hair was a mess and there were mascara tracks down her cheeks. But okay and in one piece and...safe. *Safe.*

"I'm so glad you're okay," Lia said, feeling a little out of it, but knowing that had to be said.

Sammy nodded, her own eyes filling with tears. "He stabbed you. He choked you. That's what I heard the police say."

"And I'm alive and well." Lia held out her hands for Sammy to put hers in. When she did, Lia squeezed and forced her mouth to curve. "I'd do anything to keep you safe, Sammy."

Sammy nodded, a few tears slipping over. "Can I hug you?"

Lia held her arms out. Probably a bad idea, but she didn't care. She pulled Sammy into a hug and held her close, a few tears of her own slipping out.

"I love you, Lia," Sammy whispered, resting her cheek on Lia's shoulder.

Lia's voice was already hoarse, and her throat ached even over the pain medicine, but she forced herself to say the words back anyway. "I love you too." Then she closed her eyes and just held on for a while. "You know, I'm grateful every day you decided to steal from me."

Sammy choked out a laugh, then sniffled, pulling back and wiping her cheeks with her sleeve. "Me too."

They just stared at each other for a few more minutes, like they both needed that visual reassurance that nothing catastrophic had happened. They were both going to be okay and life was going to go back to normal. Back to *good.*

But then Sammy's expression got really serious.

"It wasn't Mom's fault. It really wasn't. They tricked her. I know how I sound, and I know she was using again, but they *did* trick her. I saw it. I saw..."

Sammy was so desperate for it to be true, and it really didn't matter if it was or wasn't. "I believe you, sweetheart."

"Really?" Sammy looked at the ground. "Uncle Gard won't. He's going to be mad at her. That she…did all this. Got messed up with those guys. Got back into drugs."

"No, you underestimate him." God, it hurt to talk more than move, but Lia made herself say the words Sammy needed to hear. "Maybe he'll be a little hurt that…your mom felt desperate when he would have done anything to help her, but he's not going to blame her. He's not going to be *mad*. You know him better than that."

After a few moments of maybe letting those words soak in, Sammy nodded. Then she just looked at Lia for a long time, those blue eyes shiny with more tears. "You saved me, Lia. He was going to…" She shook her head. "You saved me."

"And Gard saved me. That makes us pretty close to even."

Sammy let out a shaky breath, still studying Lia's face. "You love him, don't you?" As she voiced that question, the door behind Sammy opened and Lia's gaze met Gard's as he stepped into the room.

He had streaks of black on his shirt, mud caked on his shoes, and his eyes were a little red-rimmed, likely from the smoke. But he was here and whole and…all that love Sammy had just asked her about swamped her.

She didn't know if he'd heard the question or not, but she didn't care. She held his intent blue gaze while she answered Sammy. "I do."

Gard was buffeted by too many feelings to really absorb any of them. But Lia looking him dead in the eye and answering Sammy's question cut through them all.

She was here. She was okay.

And she loved him.

"He loves you too," Sammy said to Lia, clearly not aware he'd walked into the room, because she said it a little desperately, like it was Sammy's job to convince Lia it was true.

Lia's mouth curved a little bit. She ran a hand over Sammy's tangled hair, but she still looked at Gard. "You think so?"

"I do," he answered for Sammy.

Sammy whirled around quick enough Gard was a little afraid she might have hurt Lia, but Lia didn't flinch.

Then, even though Sammy's eyes were full of tears, she grinned at him. "I guess you're not so dumb then."

"Guess not," he agreed, moving over to where Sammy stood, and Lia sat on the bed.

She was still pale, but they'd cleaned her up some. There was already bruising on her neck it killed him to look at. To remember the way her eyes had been wide with fear while he'd held a gun on the guy holding her, all too close for any kind of comfort.

But she loved him. And wasn't that a hell of a thing after all this?

So he looked at Sammy. "Are you supposed to be in here?" he asked disapprovingly. "Because I know *I'm* not." He'd snuck in, with a little help from Deputy Morris.

"Have you seen Mom?" Sammy asked without answering his question.

Gard shook his head. "They were running some tests. We should be able to see her soon though. Sarabeth and Izzy are in the waiting room. You don't have to see them if you're not ready, but I know they're both really worried about you."

"I want to see them. I… I didn't mean to scare them. I wish…"

Gard reached out to squeeze her shoulder and she took in a careful inhale, like she was pulling herself together.

"But it's okay. It's all okay. I'll go talk to them, but you'll stay with Lia, right?"

Gard ran a hand over Sammy's mussed hair. "I'll stay. Straight to the waiting room, and nowhere else, got it?"

Sammy nodded. She gave Lia one last gentle hug then gave Gard a harder more impulsive one before she left the room.

Gard let out a slow breath. Everything inside of him felt far too tight. But everything was…okay. They still didn't know the extent of Dani's injuries, but she was going to make it. One way or another. And since he couldn't see her yet, he focused on the woman sitting on the bed in front of him.

Who loved him. Who'd saved Sammy, at express injury to herself. He wasn't sure he'd ever fully be over that.

He eased himself into a sitting position next to Lia on her bed. Then with every last ounce of gentleness he had in him, very carefully drew her to him. He pressed a gentle kiss to her mouth, his hand behind her head even more gentle.

She sighed, relaxing into him. For a few, quiet moments, they just sat there like that. Absorbing the relief that it was over, and they were all okay.

"What would we have done without you, Lia?" he asked hoarsely, because… He couldn't imagine it. Everything that had gone right tonight had been because of her—her past, what she'd seen, done. There was no way he would have found Dani in time without her or gotten Sammy out with so few scars.

"You don't have to worry about that," she replied. Her voice didn't sound right.

He pulled back a little, studying her face and worrying. "What's the prognosis?" he asked, trying not to stare at the bruises on her neck.

"Just waiting to get the stitches in my side. No big deal. Bruised windpipe will heal on its own. I'm okay." She met his gaze and said the rest with that quiet determination she'd had all night. "I'd have suffered through a million times worse to make sure she was okay."

"I know," Gard said, everything inside of him tied painfully tight. He'd have done the same. For the both of them. But it just wrecked him she'd been the one to pay the price when she'd already been through so much.

"And I wasn't saying that just for Sammy's sake," he said, gently running a hand over her hair. "I do love you. I was going to tell you earlier but everything…went to hell."

She chuckled, then winced a little. "Yeah, I was going to tell you earlier too. And about…my past. I really was."

It meant something, he supposed. That she'd decided to tell him even before it had become necessary to save Sammy. That she'd been ready to share that, even if they hadn't been given the chance to have that organic conversation.

Maybe it was even better that way, because now that they'd been through all this he didn't know how to be anything but grateful she'd had the knowledge to keep Sammy safe.

And he remembered the guilt in her voice, when she'd talked about helping the FBI take down a group, considered it survival over anything noble. But Gard knew it *had* been noble, and he'd do everything in his power to prove that to her.

A knock sounded on the door, and then a doctor peeked her head in. "Ready to get stitched up?"

Lia nodded. "Yes." She looked at Gard. "You should go check on Sammy."

But he turned to the doctor. "Can I stay?"

She considered, then nodded. "Sure. If Ms. Blair wants you to."

He turned to Lia with a questioning expression. Her eyes were shiny again, but she didn't cry. She just nodded.

So he held her hand while the doctor stitched her up. Because they were in this together now.

For good.

Gard didn't let her be alone for even a second. If he went to go check on Dani, he made sure Sammy was by her side. Eventually, Lia got cleared to be released, and Gard took care of everything.

She'd fielded texts from Franny, since Royal had clued her friend into what had happened. But since Lia was exhausted, she didn't want any visitors. Any fuss. She just wanted to go home. Gard and Sammy could stay if they wanted to, but she wanted her bed and sleep. Rest.

She dozed in the back seat of Gard's truck, loopy and fuzzy from the painkillers, assuming they were heading for Hope Town. When she blinked her eyes open, she realized they'd arrived.

Not at her house, but his.

He came around to the passenger side and helped her out while Sammy rushed up to the front door and unlocked it.

"What about Dani?" Lia asked.

"She has to stay a little while longer in the hospital. She wanted me to take Sammy home, try to get her to rest some. I couldn't argue with that. I'll go back in a few hours. If she's not released later today, we'll figure something else out."

When he said *later today*, Lia realized it was morning, and the sun was starting to rise as she walked into Gard's house. The sky was a kind of glowy shade of pink, pretty and…hopeful.

"Why don't I make you something to eat," Sammy said when they helped her inside.

Lia's stomach wasn't up for it, thanks to the drugs, but more, she thought of that horrible cheese sauce the last time Sammy had been in that kitchen. She wouldn't be able to choke down a bite today. "I think I just want to sleep. You should sleep too, sweetheart. We all should."

"Okay. You can sleep in my bed! I have fresh sheets. I'll go get everything ready for you." Sammy practically ran down the hall.

"Not quite what I had in mind," Gard grumbled. "But she'll be happy being able to fuss over you." He smiled at Lia and Lia could only stand there feeling so absolutely overwhelmed.

He was just such a good guy. A good uncle or guardian or whatever. A good everything. And he was taking care of her and…

"I love you. I love her. I feel so lucky, even with stitches."

He pressed a kiss to her temple. "Maybe it's just the painkillers," he joked.

But it wasn't.

A few tears spilled over her cheeks, and she sniffled. "You gave me a family, Gard." This thing she felt like she'd never really had, was suddenly…real and hers. One she'd made. One she'd fight to keep.

He stroked a gentle hand down her cheek, wiping the

tears away. "You helped make us a family, Lia." He pressed a gentle kiss to her temple.

Lia knew it wouldn't be smooth sailing from here on out—Dani would have to go to some kind of recovery, and Sammy would need to deal with that and what had happened to her.

But they were a family now, so they *would* deal.

No matter what.

Epilogue

Sammy's sweet sixteen party was *almost* as fun as Sarabeth's had been six months earlier, at least in Sammy's estimation. She wished *she* had a ranch and horses like Sarabeth, but she'd settled for a cupcake-decorating party at the bakery, followed by a picnic out at the Hope Town park.

Gard had barbecued and a bunch of Lia's friends had brought sides and Lia had made a wonderfully amazing birthday cake decorated with all of Sammy's favorite things.

All of Sammy's friends had come. Izzy and Sarabeth, a couple kids from the debate team, and a girl from her English class.

And Mom. Who was currently sitting next to Lia while Sammy opened her presents. Mom and Lia got along really well, and every time Sammy saw it, her heart felt too big for her chest. It was like…all the bad stuff last year had led to all this really good stuff.

They'd all agreed that it would be best if Sammy stayed with Gard while she finished high school. With her rehab done, Mom was living on her own for a little bit so she could really focus on getting better.

Mom got to visit whenever she wanted, and sometimes Sammy went to lunch or dinner with her all alone. The only thing Sammy wasn't allowed to do was spend the night with Mom, and she was okay with that.

Sammy was being very…realistic about her mom's recovery. Maybe it would last. Maybe it wouldn't. But she was going to enjoy this time Mom was clean while she could. And it was easier, knowing that Mom's last relapse had been more complicated than just wanting to get high.

Therapy helped too, she guessed.

And Lia. Who was like having a…not another mom, but someone just as important. Just like Gard. An anchor. A foundation.

Sammy didn't know why they hadn't moved in together yet, but sometimes Lia stayed at their house in Bent. Sometimes Lia had Sammy spend the night with her—just her, and Lia loved those nights when it was just the two of them.

But she loved every time it was the three of them too. Or the four of them. Sometimes in her life, Sammy had felt fully and completely alone.

She almost never did these days.

Sammy had let her real hair color grow out since that night—so it was a dirty blond right now, but Lia had convinced Gard to let her dye it purple. Which he was really going to have to approve of, because when Sammy opened her gift from Lia, it was a certificate to a hair place in Fairmont.

Sammy thanked her with a big hug.

What more could she want?

"I think that's it," Sammy said, looking around the debris of all the presents. Her heart still felt too big in her chest, like this was all too much. Like she didn't deserve it, but Matilda said she wasn't supposed to worry about *deserving*.

She was supposed to work on gratitude, and Sammy *was* grateful. For everything in this perfect moment.

"Not *quite*," Gard said, getting to his feet. He walked

away from the little pavilion much to Sammy's confusion. She looked at Lia and Mom, who were both grinning.

Then she heard a *yip*. Her heart just…*stopped*. Gard reappeared with a little ball of fur in his arms.

Tears filled Sammy's eyes. Fell over her cheeks before she even touched the puppy. But they were happy tears. The best, most wonderful happy tears.

Gard put the dog in her arms, where it wriggled and licked excitably.

Grateful didn't begin to cover it.

"Happy birthday, Sammy," he said, running a hand over her hair while she cradled the wriggling puppy to her chest.

"What's his name?" she asked in between totally embarrassing sobs, but she didn't care when the puppy licked the tears off her face.

"It's a her, and she's yours to name."

Sammy gave it a lot of thought as she went through the rest of her party. She consulted Sarabeth and Izzy and never let the puppy out of her sight.

As people started to leave, and Gard, Lia, and Mom started to clean up, Sammy still hadn't made a decision, but she held the puppy's leash and led her to a patch of grass when Izzy told her that it looked like she was ready to go to the bathroom.

Izzy was an expert. The puppy had come from one of her dad's dogs, so she was bred to be smart.

"You're going to be a genius, aren't you?" Sammy cooed at the dog. She turned back toward the pavilion where all the adults in her life cleaned up. She kind of felt bad she wasn't helping, but Gard had said it was her birthday so she didn't have to.

She had gratitude for that too.

He was over cleaning the grill while Mom and Lia picked

up trash and packed up leftover food. As Sammy walked past them, she heard a little snippet of their conversation.

"Thank you," Mom was saying, low and serious. "For being what she needed. What she *needs*."

Lia reached out and gave Mom's arm a squeeze. "Aren't we lucky that she needs us both?"

Hearing that made Sammy want to cry again, because it was true and she knew *she* was lucky that Lia understood how much they both meant to Sammy.

Which just meant that this birthday party shouldn't *only* be about her. She made a beeline for Gard, the puppy chewing on her leash as she did.

"Gard."

"What's up?" he asked, closing the lid on the grill and tossing some crumpled-up foil into the trash can.

"I have one more thing to ask for my birthday."

He shook his head, looking sidelong at the puppy. "Getting a little late in the day, kid." He pointed at the dog. "And that's already one pretty big ask right there. Lia's the one who thinks we can make it work."

"She's right," Sammy said emphatically. "So now is the perfect time to ask her."

He put on that poker face. Lia called it his *cop* face. Lia was right. "Ask her what?" he replied.

Sammy rolled her eyes at him. She'd helped him pick out the ring, so he couldn't pretend he didn't know what she was talking about.

He sighed at her pointed look. "It's your party, Sammy. I'll do it soon enough."

"Do it now. Just ask her. *Please.* You have the ring, so why not?" She knew he'd picked it up this morning when he'd been doing errands for the party. Which meant he *had* it.

Lia was going to love it. Sammy didn't have any doubts. Not about rings or her uncle getting married or Lia. Not *one*.

Gard glanced over at where Lia was taking down streamers. Even his cop face softened.

"Please," Sammy added, almost positive she was winning.

He sighed. "Fine, but if she says no in front of you, you only have yourself to blame."

He was trying to make a joke, but Sammy watched with some amusement as he wiped his palms on his jeans like he was nervous. Sammy nearly bounded all the way over to Mom.

"Lia," Gard said. "Can you come down here for a second?"

Lia looked down at him from where she stood on the picnic table pulling down the last of the balloons. She frowned a little at him but let him help her down so they were on equal footing.

"I didn't exactly plan on having an audience for this," he said, keeping her hand in his. "But someone insisted." He jutted his chin toward Sammy. Sammy had to sit on her hands to keep from clapping them together. She bounced in her seat next to Mom.

Lia looked utterly baffled. "An audience for what?"

Sammy grabbed her mom's hand and squeezed to keep from excitably saying something.

Gard got down on one knee, and Lia's confusion turned to shock. Her gaze flew to Sammy, and Sammy nodded emphatically, feeling tears sting her eyes.

She thought about what Lia had told her a long time ago. That pursuing and enjoying and surrounding yourself with the things and people you loved helped ease the aches of bad feelings. That it was better than trying to save yourself from hurt.

She'd been right.

"Lia, I love you," Gard said, his low voice gruff and earnest. "You make my life immeasurably better. Will you marry me, even though I'm asking you in front of my sister and my niece?"

She laughed. That was the best part, Sammy thought. Gard and Lia made each other laugh. Made each other happy. And now they would forever, Sammy was sure of it.

Lia sank down onto her knees and put her arms around Gard's neck. Whatever she said to him, Sammy couldn't hear, but she knew it was a yes.

Of course it was a yes.

"They're perfect for each other, aren't they?" Mom whispered, giving Sammy a little squeeze.

"They are," Sammy agreed, leaning into her mother.

And she patted herself on the back for all those months ago. Trying to steal from Lia had been the best worst thing she'd ever done.

Because it had turned out all right, hadn't it? She knelt down and picked up the puppy into her arms again.

More than all right, in fact.

The absolute best.

* * * * *

Don't miss Hunted in Hope Town *by Nicole Helm
the next thrilling installment of her new miniseries
Hope Town Secrets
On sale August 2026,
Wherever Harlequin books and ebooks are sold.*

Get up to 4 Free Books!

We'll send you 2 free books from each series you try
PLUS a free Mystery Gift.

Both the **Harlequin Intrigue®** and **Harlequin® Romantic Suspense** series feature compelling novels filled with heart-racing action-packed romance that will keep you on the edge of your seat.

YES! Please send me 2 FREE novels from the Harlequin Intrigue or Harlequin Romantic Suspense series and my FREE gift (gift is worth about $10 retail). I may cancel anytime by emailing ReaderServiceInfo@Harlequin.com or by calling 1-800-873-8635. If I don't cancel, I will receive 6 brand-new Harlequin Intrigue Larger-Print books every month and be billed just $7.19 each in the U.S. or $7.99 each in Canada, or 4 brand-new Harlequin Romantic Suspense books every month and be billed just $6.39 each in the U.S. or $7.19 each in Canada, a savings of 20% off the cover price. It's quite a bargain! Shipping and handling is just 75¢ per book in the U.S. and $1.75 per book in Canada.* I understand that accepting the free books and gift places me under no obligation to buy anything—they are mine to keep for free no matter what I decide.

Choose one:
☐ **Harlequin Intrigue Larger-Print** (199/399 BPA G3CD)
☐ **Harlequin Romantic Suspense** (240/340 BPA G3CD)
☐ **Or Try Both!** (199/399 & 240/340 BPA G3CE)

Name (please print)

Address

Apt. #

City

State/Province

Zip/Postal Code

Email: Please check this box ☐ if you would like to receive newsletters and promotional emails from Harlequin Enterprises ULC and its affiliates. You can unsubscribe anytime.

Mail to the Harlequin Reader Service:
IN U.S.A.: P.O. Box 1341, Buffalo, NY 14240-8531
IN CANADA: P.O. Box 603, Fort Erie, Ontario L2A 5X3

Want to explore our other series or interested in ebooks? **Visit www.ReaderService.com or call 1-800-873-8635.**

*Terms and prices subject to change without notice. Prices do not include sales taxes, which will be charged (if applicable) based on your state or country of residence. Canadian residents will be charged applicable taxes. Offer not valid in Quebec. This offer is limited to one order per household. Books received may not be as shown. Not valid for current subscribers to the Harlequin Intrigue or Harlequin Romantic Suspense series. All orders subject to approval. Credit or debit balances in a customer's account(s) may be offset by any other outstanding balance owed by or to the customer. Please allow 4 to 6 weeks for delivery. Offer available while quantities last.

Your Privacy — Your information is being collected by Harlequin Enterprises ULC, operating as Harlequin Reader Service. For a complete summary of the information we collect, how we use this information and to whom it is disclosed, please visit our privacy notice located at https://corporate.harlequin.com/privacy-notice. Notice to California Residents—Under California law, you have specific rights to control and access your data. For more information on these rights and how to exercise them, visit https://corporate.harlequin.com/california-privacy. For additional information for residents of other U.S. states that provide their residents with certain rights with respect to personal data, visit https://corporate.harlequin.com/other-state-residents-privacy-rights.

HIHRS2603